John Pinkerton

Select Scottish Ballads

Volume I

John Pinkerton

Select Scottish Ballads
Volume I

ISBN/EAN: 9783744766654

Printed in Europe, USA, Canada, Australia, Japan

Cover: Foto ©Andreas Hilbeck / pixelio.de

More available books at **www.hansebooks.com**

SELECT

SCOTISH BALLADS.

VOLUME I.

CONTAINING

BALLADS

IN THE

TRAGIC STYLE.

THE SECOND EDITION,
CORRECTED AND ENLARGED.

SELECT

SCOTISH BALLADS.

VOLUME I.

P. 28.

LONDON,
PRINTED BY AND FOR J. NICHOLS.
MDCCLXXXIII.

HARDYKNUTE,

AN HEROIC BALLAD,

NOW FIRST PUBLISHED COMPLETE;

WITH THE OTHER MORE APPROVED

SCOTISH BALLADS,

AND SOME NOT HITHERTO MADE PUBLIC,

IN THE TRAGIC STYLE.

TO WHICH ARE PREFIXED

TWO DISSERTATIONS,

I. ON THE ORAL TRADITION OF POETRY.
II. ON THE TRAGIC BALLAD.

JAMQUE SACRUM TENERIS VATEM VENERETUR AB ANNIS.

TO HIS GRACE THE Duke of BUCCLEUGH.

MY LORD,

IT is with much pleaſure I embrace this opportunity of teſtifying my ſincere reſpect for YOUR GRACE's exalted character, as the friend and as the ornament of your country, by addreſſing theſe volumes to a name ſo much revered and beloved by the nation whoſe poetry they are intended to preſerve and to illuſtrate.

The chief compoſitions in this volume, My Lord, will be found to breathe the living ſpirit of the Scotiſh people, a race of men who have left monuments of their martial glory in every country. Your Grace, it is hoped, will with pleaſure here recogniſe the noble ardour your example lately tended to revive, by raiſing and commanding in perſon a military force in defence of your country, at a period when her natives had not diſcernment to perceive, nor ſpirit to aſſume, the privileges of Britiſh ſubjects.

The ſecond volume, My Lord, contains chiefly pieces deſcriptive of rural merriment, and of love and domeſtic happineſs. Even theſe, it is humbly believed, Your Grace will not diſdain; for it is well known that the felicity of the poor in general, and of your numerous tenants and dependants in particular,

particular, is regarded by YOUR GRACE as eſſential to your own. In reward, YOUR GRACE enjoys a domeſtic felicity now ſeldom or never known to the great, who are generally obliged to exchange the free enjoyment of true pleaſure for the gaudy ſlavery of oſtentation.

At a period when many of the Britiſh nobility are waſting their patrimonial eſtates in profligate diſſipation; men trained to arms in defence of their rights and liberties, villages beautified and rendered ſalubrious, and their inhabitants rendered happy, have been the monuments of expence of the DUKE OF BUCCLEUGH.

The ſilent gratitude of the poor will ever ſpeak YOUR GRACE's praiſes with an expreſſion unknown to the moſt exalted elocution; and it were ſurely abſurd for any writer to enlarge on what is the common ſubject

of

of converſation, and known to all; I ſhall not therefore any longer intrude on YOUR GRACE's patience.

That SCOTLAND may long conſider YOUR GRACE as one of the beſt guardians of her liberty, and the living aſſertor of her ancient ſpirit, is the earneſt wiſh of,

MY LORD,

YOUR GRACE's

Moſt obedient Servant,

JOHN PINKERTON.

CONTENTS.

16. *Laird*

DISSERTATIONS

ON THE

ORAL TRADITION OF POETRY,

AND ON

THE TRAGIC BALLAD.

DISSERTATION I.

ON THE ORAL TRADITION OF POETRY.

IT has long been a subject of regret, that the inventors of the fine Arts have by oblivion been deprived of the reputation due to their memory. Of the many realms which lay claim to their birth, Egypt seems to possess the preference. Yet, like the Nile, which animates that country, while they have diffused pleasure and utility over kingdoms, their origin remains hid in the most profound obscurity.

That poetry holds a distinguished superiority over all these sciences is allowed; yet the first practiser of this enchanting art has lost the renown it was designed to confer. We must either allow the contested claim of the Osiris of the Egyptians, and Apollo of the Greeks, or be content to withhold from any, the fame which indeed seems due to as many inventors as there are distinct nations in the world. For poetry appears not to require the labour of disquisition, or aid of chance, to invent; but is rather the original language of men in an infant state of society in all countries. It is the effusion of fancy actuated by the passions: and that these are always strongest when uncontrouled by custom, and the manners which in an advanced community are termed polite, is evident. But the peculiar advantages, which a certain situation of extrinsic objects confers on this art, have already been so well illustrated by eminent critics *, that it is unnecessary here to remember them. I have besides noted a few such as immediately concern the compositions now under view in the subsequent Dissertation; and only propose here to give a brief account of the utility of the Oral Tradition of Poetry, in that barbarous state of society which necessarily precedes the invention of letters; and of the circumstances that conspired to render it easy and safe.

Among the Egyptians, probably the most ancient authors of the elegant, as well as useful sciences, we find that verses were originally used solely to preserve the laws of their princes, and sayings of their wise men from oblivion †. These were sometimes inscribed in their temples in their hieroglyphic character, but more

* Particularly Dr. Blackwell, in his Enquiry into the Life and Writings of Homer; and Dr. Blair, in his elegant Dissertation on the Poems of Ossian.

† Herodot. Diodor. Sicul. &c.

frequently only committed to the memory of the expounders of their Law, or disciples of their sages. Pythagoras, who was initiated in their secret science, conveyed in like manner his dictates to his disciples, as appears from the moral verses which pass under his name at this day. And though the authenticity of these may be questioned, yet that he followed this mode of bequeathing his knowledge to his followers, is proved from the consent of all antiquity *. Nay, before him, Thales composed in like manner his System of Natural Philosophy. And even so late as the time of Aristotle, the Laws of the Agathyrsi, a nation in Sarmatia, were all delivered in verse. Not to mention the known laws of the Twelve Tables, which, from the fragments still remaining of them, appear to have consisted of short rythmic sentences.

From laws and religion poetry made an easy progress to the celebration of the Gods and Heroes, who were their founders. Verses in their praise were sung on solemn occasions by the composers, or bards themselves. We meet with many before Homer, who distinguished themselves by such productions. Fabricius † has enumerated near seventy whose names have reached our times. That immortal author had the advantage of

* Jamblichus de vita Pythag. *passim*; and particularly *lib.* I. *cap.* 15. and 25.

† In Bibliotheca Græca, *tom.* I.

hearing their poems repeated; and was certainly indebted to his predecessors for many beauties which we admire as original. That he was himself an ΑΟΙΔΟΣ, or Minstrel, and sung his own verses to the lyre, is shown by the admirable author of the Enquiry into his Life and Writings *. Nor were his poems rescued from the uncertain fame of tradition, and committed to writing till some time after his death †.

Such was the utility of the poetic tradition among the more polished nations of antiquity: and with those they denominated Barbarians we find it no less practised ‡. The Persians had their Magi, who preserved, as would seem in this way, the remarkable events of former times, and in war went before the army singing the praises of their illustrious men, whom the extraordinary gratitude and admiration of their countrymen had exalted into Deities. If they gained the victory, the Song of Triumph recorded the deeds of those who had fallen, and by their praises animated the ambition of those who enjoyed the conquest to farther acts of valour. The latter custom

* Sect. VIII.

† Ælian. Var. Hist. lib. xiii. c. 14.

‡ The reader, who would desire more intelligence on this head, may consult a curious *Dissertation on the Monuments which supplied the Defect of Writing among the first Historians*, by the Abbé Anselm, in Les Memoires de l'Academie des Inscriptions, &c.

was in uſe ſtill more anciently among the Jews, as appears from the ſongs of Moſes * and Deborah † preſerved in Sacred Writ.

The Druids of Gaul and Britain afford a noted inſtance ‡. Such firm hold did their traditions take of the memory, that ſome of them are retained in the minds of their countrymen to this very day §. The

* Exod XV. † Judges V.

‡ Et Bardi quidem fortia virorum illuſtrium facta heroicis compoſita verſibus, cum dulcibus lyræ modulis cantitarunt. *Ammian. Marcell.* lib. xvi.

§ Atque horum (Bardorum ſeu Druidarum) cantiones, aut ad ſimilitudinem potius earundem fictæ etiamnum aliquæ extant *die Meiſter Geſänge*, ſed recentiores pleræque, nec vel quingentos annos excedentes. *Beſſel. in notis ad Eginhart.* Traject. 1711, *p.* 130. Nonnulli eruditi viri obſervarunt veterem illam Gallorum conſuetudinem (*ſcil.* viſci ſacrum uſum apud druidas) etiam nunc multis Galliæ locis retineri, cum anni initio clamitant, *Au guy l'an neuf.* i. e. Ad viſcum; annus novus. *Hotoman. ad Cæſ. l.* 6. Druydes vero Heduorum, qui tunc habitabant in quodam loco, hodiernis temporibus Mons druidum dictus, diſtans a noſtra civitate Heduenſi per unum milliare ubi adhuc reſtant veſtigia loci habitationis eorum, utebantur pro eorum armis anguibus in campo azureo; habebant etiam in parte ſuperiore ramum viſci quercinei (*ung rameaul de guyg de chaſne*) et in parte inferiore unum cumulum parvorum anguium ſeu ſerpentium argenteorum quaſi tunc naſcentium, qui vulgo dicitur, *coubce de ſerpens d'argent.* *Chaſſeneux* Catalogi Gloriæ mundi, 1529, *folio verſo* 26.

 Germans,

Germans, as we learn from Tacitus, had no other mode of commemorating the tranſactions of paſt times than by verſe. The brave actions of their anceſtors were always ſung as an incentive to their imitation before they entered into combat. The like we read of the ancient Goths *, thoſe deſtroyers of all literature, who yet poſſeſſed greater ſkill in the fine arts than is commonly aſcribed to them. From them this cuſtom paſſed to their deſcendants the inhabitants of the Northern regions, many animated ſpecimens of whoſe traditional poetry have been preſerved to our times † and quoted by their modern hiſtorians as uncontroulable vouchers; as the Arabian hiſtorians refer for the truth of many events to the Spaniſh romanzes, ſaved in like manner by tradition for many ages, many of which are of very remote antiquity, and abound with the higher beauties of poetry ‡. Traditional verſes are to this day a favourite amuſement of the Mahometan nations; though, inſtead of recording the illuſtrious actions of their real heroes, they chaunt the fabled exploits of

* Jornand. See *Warton's Hiſt. of Engliſh Poetry.*

† See the Hiſtories of Saxo Grammat. Jo. Magnus, Torfæus, &c. *paſſim*; and Dr. Percy's *Five Pieces of Runic Poetry.*

‡ *Hiſt. de las guerras civiles de Granada.* A moſt beautiful imitation of their manner may be found among the Poems of Voiture. The Spaniſh word *Romanze* ſeems now applied to any ſhort lyric tale on whatever ſubject. We find in Gongora, their moſt eminent poet, *Romances Amoroſos, y Burleſcos.*

Buhalul

Buhalul their Orlando *, or the yet more ridiculous ones of their Prophet †. From them it would appear that rime, that great help to the remembrance of traditional poetry, passed to the Troubadours of Provence; who from them seem also to have received the spirit and character of their effusions. Like them, they composed amorous verses with delicacy and nature; but when they attempted the sublimer walk of the Heroic Song, their imagination was often bewildered, and they wandered into the contiguous regions of the incredible and absurd ‡.

In proportion as Literature advanced in the world, Oral Tradition disappeared. The venerable British Bards were in time succeeded by the Welsh Beirdh §,

* Huet, Lettre à Monsieur Segrais, sur l'origine des Romans, p. LXVII. edit. d'Amst. 1715.

† Historiale description de l'Afrique, escrite de notre temps par Jean Leon, African, premierement en langue Arabesque, puis en Toscane, et à present mise en François—En Anvers, 1556. *lib.* III. *p.* 175.

A curious specimen of the Eastern religious poetry may be seen in Sir John Chardin's Voyage to Persia, vol. I.

‡ Huet, ubi supra, p. LXX. Ermengarde vicomtesse de Narbonne——L'accueil favorable qu'elle fit aux Poetes Provençeaux, a fait croire qu'elle tenoit cour *d'amour* dans son Palais, mourot 1194. Almanach Historique de Languedoc, à Toulouse, 1752, p. 277. See Hist. Liter. des Troub. *Paris*, 1774. Translations of Provenzal Sirventes, and an imitation of the Provenzal Heroic Romanze, may be found in a volume lately published by Mr. Dilly, intituled, RIMES. Odes, Book II. Odes, 8, 9, 10, 11, 12, 13. 16.

§ History of Wales, by Caradoc of Lhancarvan, &c. 1702. p. 159

whoſe principal occupation ſeems to have been to preſerve the genealogy of their patrons, or at times to amuſe them with ſome fabulous ſtory of their predeceſſors ſung to the harp or crowd *, an inſtrument which Griffith ap Conan, King of Wales, is ſaid to have brought from Ireland, about the beginning of the twelfth century.

In like manner, among the Caledonians, as an ingenious writer † acquaints us, "Every chief in proceſs "of time had a bard in his family, and the office be"came hereditary. By the ſucceſſion of theſe bards the "poems concerning the anceſtors of the family were "handed down from generation to generation; they "were repeated to the whole clan on ſolemn occa"ſions, and always alluded to in the new compoſi"tions of the bards." The ſucceſſors of Oſſian were at length employed chiefly in the mean office of preſerving fabulous genealogies, and flattering the pride of their chieftains at the expence of truth, without

* This is the inſtrument meant in the following verſes of Ven. Fortunatus, lib. vii.

Romanuſque lyra plaudat tibi, barbarus harpa,
Græcus Achilliaca, Crotta Britanna canat.

See more of the Harp in War. Antiq. Hibern. cap. 22. And Mr. Evans, Diſſert. de Bardis, p. 80.

† Mr. Macpherſon, in his Diſſertation on the Era of Oſſian, p. 228. ed. 1773.

even

even fancy ſufficient to render their inventions either pleaſing or plauſible. That order of men, I believe, is now altogether extinct; yet they have left a ſpirit of poetry in the country where they flouriſhed *; and Oſſian's harp ſtill yields a dying ſound among the wilds of Morven.'

Having thus given a faint view of the progreſs of the Oral Tradition of Poetry to theſe times †, I proceed to ſhew what arts the ancient bards employed to make their verſes take ſuch hold of the memory of their countrymen, as to be tranſmitted ſafe and entire without the aid of writing for many ages. Theſe may be conſidered as affecting the paſſions and the ear. Their mode of expreſſion was ſimple and genuine. They of conſequence touched the paſſions truly and effectively. And when the paſſions are engaged, we liſten with avidity to the tale that ſo agreeably affects them; and remember it again with the moſt prompt facility. This may be obſerved in children, who will forget no circumſtance of an intereſting ſtory, more eſpecially if ſtriking or dreadful to the fancy; when they cannot remember a ſhort maxim which only occupies the judgement. The paſſions of men have been and will be the ſame through all ages. Poetry is the ſovereign of the paſſions, and will reign while they

* See Martin's, and other Deſcriptions of the Weſtern Iſles, paſſim.

† For an account of the more modern minſtrels ſee Dr. Percy's Diſſertation, which is ſo complete that it leaves nothing to add.

exiſt. We may laugh at Sir Iſaac Newton, as we have at Deſcartes; but we ſhall always admire a Homer, an Oſſian, or a Shakſpere.

As the ſubjects of theſe genuine painters of nature deeply intereſted the heart, and by that means were ſo agreeable and affecting, that every hearer wiſhed to remember them; ſo their mode of conſtructing their verſe was ſuch, that the remembrance was eaſy and expeditious. A few of their many arts to aid the memory I ſhall here enumerate.

I. Moſt of theſe Oral poems were ſet to muſic, as would appear, by the original authors themſelves. That this was the cuſtom ſo early as the days of Homer, may be ſeen in the excellent author formerly adduced *. How ſhould we have been affected by hearing a compoſition of Homer or Oſſian ſung and played by theſe immortal maſters themſelves! With the poem the air ſeems to have paſſed from one age to another; but as no muſical compoſitions of the Greeks exiſt, we are quite in the dark as to the nature of theſe. I ſuppoſe that Oſſian's poetry is ſtill recited to its original cadence and to appropriated tunes. We find, in an excellent modern writer †, that this mode of ſinging poetry to the harp was reckoned an accompliſhment ſo late as among the Saxon Eccleſiaſtics. The ancient

* Enquiry, &c. Sect. VIII.

† Mr. Warton, in his Hiſtory of Engliſh Poetry.

muſic

music was confessedly infinitely superior to ours in the command of the passions. Nay, the music of the most barbarous countries has had effects that not all the sublime pathos of Corelli, or animated strains of Handel, could produce. Have not the Welsh, Irish, and Scotish tunes, greater influence over the most informed mind at this day than the best Italian concerto? What Modern refined music could have the powers of the *Rance de Vaches* * of the Swiss, or the melancholy sound of the Indian Bansha †? Is not the war-music of the rudest inhabitants of the wilds of America or Scotland more terrible to the ear than that of the best band in the British army? Or, what is still more surprizing, will not the softer passions be more inflamed by a

* See Rousseau, Dict. de Musique, *sur cette article*. Though the Swiss are a brave nation, yet their dance, which corresponds to the *Rance des Vaches*, is, like their others, rather expressive of an effeminate spirit. 'Les dances des Suisses consistent en un continuel 'trainement de Jambe, ces pas repondoient mal au courage ferme 'de cette nation. Coquillart en son Blazon des armes, et des dames.'

'Les Escossoys sont les repliques,
'Pragois et Bretons bretonnans,
'Les Suisses dancent leurs Moresques,
'A touts leurs tabourins sonnans.'

Mons. L. D. Notes à Rabelais, Tom. IV. p. 164. 1725.

† See Grainger's Proso-poetic Account of the Culture of the Sugar-cane, Book IV.

Turkish

Turkish air than by the most exquisite effort of a polite composer? as we learn from an elegant writer *, whom concurring circumstances rendered the best judge that could be imagined of that subject. The harmony therefore of the old traditional songs possessing such influence over the passions, at the same time that it rendered every expression necessary to the ear, must have greatly recommended them to the remembrance.

II. Besides musical cadence, many arts were used in the versification to facilitate the rehearsal. Such were:

1. The frequent returns of the same sentences and descriptions expressed in the very same words. As for instance, the delivery of messages, the description of battles, &c. of which we meet with infinite examples in Homer, and some, if I mistake not, in Ossian. Good ones may be found in Hardyknute, Part I. v. 123, &c. compared with part II. v. 107, &c. and in Child Maurice, v. 31, with v. 67; and innumerable such in the ancient Traditional Poetry of all nations. These served as land marks, in the view of which the memory travelled secure over the intervening spaces. On this head falls likewise to be mentioned what we call The Burden, that is, the unvaried repetition of one or more lines fixing the tone of the poem throughout the whole. That this is very ancient among the barbaric nations, may be gathered from the known Song of Regner

* Letters of Lady M. W. Montague, XXXIII.

Lodbrog,

Lodbrog, to be found in Olaus Wormius *; every ſtanza of which begins with one and the ſame line. So many of our ballads, both ancient and modern, have this aid to the memory, that it is unneceſſary to condeſcend on any in particular.

2. Alliteration was before the invention of rime greatly uſed, chiefly by the nations of Northern original, to aſſiſt the remembrance of their traditional poetry. Moſt of the Runic methods of verſification conſiſted in this practice. It was the only one among the Saxon poets, from whom it paſſed to the Engliſh and Scotiſh †. When rime became common, this which was

* Regner Lodbrog, King of Denmark, flouriſhed in the Ninth Century.

† See Hickes, *Ling. Vet. Sept. Theſ. c.* 23. From the Saxons he obſerves, that the author of *Pierce Plowman* drew this practice, c. 21. This poem was written about 1350. There is a remarkable ſimilarity in its ſtyle and manner with thoſe very curious pieces of ancient Scotiſh poetry, ſtyled The Prophecies of Thomas Rymer, Marvellous Merling, Beid, Berlington, Waldhave, Eltraine, Baniſter, and Sybilla, printed at Edinburgh in 1615, and reprinted from that edition, 1742, 8vo. It is very ſurpriſing that the reſpectable editor of *Ancient Scottiſh Poems, from the MS. of George Bannatyne,* 1568. *Edin.* 1770, ſeems to regard theſe as not more ancient than the time of Queen Mary. His reaſons are only founded on the modern appearance of ſome particular paſſages. That they have been modernized and corrupted, I will readily allow;

was before thought to constitute the sole difference between prose and verse, was still regarded as an accessary

allow; but that they are on the main nearly as ancient as Rymer's time, who died about the beginning of the 14th Century, I believe the learned must confess from intrinsic evidence, in such cases the surest of all. Not to mention that Sir David Lindsay, who wrote in the reign of James V. is an undoubted witness that they must be more ancient than this eminent Antiquary would infer. For in enumerating the methods he took to divert that prince while under his care in his infancy, after condescending on some risible circumstances, as

When thou wast young I bare thee in my arm
Full tenderly till thou began to gang;
And in thy bed oft happed thee full warm,
With lute in hand than sweetly to thee sang,
Sometime in dancing fiercefully I flang,
And sometimes playing fairses on the flure,
And sometimes of mine office taking cure.
And sometimes like a feind transfigurate,
And sometimes like a greesy ghost of gay,
In divers forms oft times disfigurate, &c.

He adds,

The Prophesies of *Rymer*, *Bede*, and *Merlin*,
And many other pleasant history
Of the red *Erin*, and *Gyre Carlin*,
Comforting thee when that I saw thee sory.

Epistle to the King, prefixed to his Dream.

They

ſary grace, and was carried to a ludicrous length by ſome poets of no mean rank in both nations. So late

They begin thus:

Merling ſays in his book, who will read right,
Althouch his ſayings be uncouth, they ſhall be true found,
In the ſeventh chapter read who ſo will,
One thouſand and more after Chriſt's birth.
Then the Chalnalider of Cornwall is called,
And the wolf out of Wales is vanquiſhed for aye,
Then many ſerlies ſhall fall, and many folk ſhall die.

This exordium is evidently retouched by a modern hand.—But very many of the paſſages ſeem to ſtand in their original form, as the following lines, which are all in the Saxon manner, will teſtify:

And derfly dong down without any doome—
A proud prince in the preis lordly ſhall light,
With bold Barons in buſhment to battle ſhall wend.—
There ſhall a galyart goat with a golden horn.——

And many ſimilar. That prophecy which bears the name of Thomas Rymer is not deſtitute of poetic graces. It opens with the following lines:

Still on my ways as I went
Out throuch a land beſide a lee,
I met a bairn upon the bent *,
Methought him ſeemly for to ſee,

* *Modernized way, though againſt the rime.*

I asked

late as the reign of Queen Elizabeth we find the following lines in a court poet:

Princes puff'd; barons blustered; lords began lowr,
Knights storm'd; squires startled, like steeds in a stowr;
Pages and yeomen yelled out in the hall *.

And William Dunbar, the chief of the old Scotish poets, begins a copy of verses to the King thus,

Sanct Salvator send silver sorrow †.

I asked him wholly his intent;
Good Sir, if your will be,
Since that ye bide upon the bent,
Some uncouth tidings tell you me:
When shall all these wars be gone?
That leil men may live in lee;
Or when shall Fasehude go from home,
And Lawtie blow his horn on hie?
I looked from me not a mile,
And saw twa knights upon a lee, &c.

I imagine, however, they are all the composures of one hand; and, if I may use a conjecture, were written immediately after the visions of Pierce Plowman, every English poem of note in those days being soon succeeded by an imitation in Scotland.

* *King Ryence's Challenge*, in the Reliques of Ancient English Poetry. *Vol.* III. *p.* 27.

† Bannatyne's Scottish Poems, p. 68.

III. But the greatest assistance that could be found to the tradition of poetry was derived from the invention of rime; which is far more ancient than is commonly believed. One of the most learned men this age has produced *, has shewn that it is common in Scripture. All the Psalms consist of riming verses, and many other passages which he names. They were used among the Greeks so early as the time of Gorgias the Sicilian, who taught the Athenians this practice. And though the spirit of the Greek and Latin languages did not always admit of them in poetry, yet they were used as occasional beauties by their most celebrated writers. Homer, Hesiod, and Virgil, have a few, though apparently more from chance than design. The ancient Saturnine verses were all rimes, as an old commentator † informs us. And it is more than probable they were so constructed merely that the memory might the more easily preserve them, their licence forbidding their being committed to writing. Those who would wish to know more particularly the universality of this mode of versifying among the other ancient nations, may consult the *Huetiana* of the most learned and respectable Bishop of Avranches ‡. The Eastern poetry consists altogether, if I mistake not, of riming lines, as may be observed in the specimens of Hafiz their most

* Le Clerc, Biblioth. Universelle, tom. IX.

† Servius ad Georg. II. ver. 386.

‡ Sect. 78.

 illustrious

illuſtrious writer, lately publiſhed *. It appears, however, that alliteration ſupplied the place of rime with the Northern nations till within a recent period †. Oſſian's poetry, I ſuppoſe, is in ſtanzas ſomething like our ballad meaſure; though it were to be wiſhed the tranſlator had favoured us with ſome information on this head evidenced by ſpecimens of the original. He indeed acquaints us that "Each verſe was ſo connected with thoſe which preceded, or followed it, "that if one line had been remembered in a ſtanza, it "was almoſt impoſſible to forget the reſt ‡:" but this ſtands greatly in need of explanation.

The common ballad ſtanza is ſo ſimple, that it has been uſed by moſt nations as the firſt mode of conſtructing rimes. The Spaniſh romanzes bear a great reſemblance in this, as in other reſpects, to the Scotiſh Ballads. In both, every alternate line ends with ſimilar vowels, though the conſonants are not ſo ſtrictly attended to. As for inſtance, in the former we have *lana*, *eſpada*; *mala*, *palabra*; *vega*, *cueva*; *rompan*, *volcanos*; for rimes: and in the later, *middle*, *girdle*; *keep*, *bleed*; *Buleighan*, *tak him*; &c. The Engliſh, even in the ruder pieces of their firſt minſtrels, ſeem to have

* Jones, Comment. Poeſeos Aſiaticæ—Richardſon's Specimen of Perſian Poetry.

† Ol. Worm. Lit. Run. p. 165 & 176.

‡ Diſſert. on the Era of Oſſian, p. 228. ed. 1773.

 paid

paid more attention to the correſpondence of their conſonants, as may be obſerved in the curious Collection publiſhed by Dr. Percy.

As the ſimplicity of this ſtanza rendered it eaſy to the compoſer, and likewiſe more natural to expreſs the paſſions, ſo it added to the facility of recollection. It's tone is ſedate and ſlow. The rimes occur ſeldom, and at equal diſtances: though when a more violent paſſion is to be painted, by doubling the rimes, they at once expreſſed the mind better, and diverſified the harmony. Of this the reader will obſerve many inſtances in this collection, as, *Here maun I lie, here maun I die: Like beacon bricht at deid of nicht: Na river heir, my dame deir:* &c. and, to give a very ſolemn movement to the cadence, they ſometimes tripled the rime, an inſtance of which may be obſerved in the firſt ſtanza of Child Maurice.

When all the circumſtances here hinted at are conſidered, we ſhall be leſs apt to wonder, that, by the concurrence of muſical air, retentive arts in the compoſition, and chiefly of rime, the moſt noble productions of former periods have been preſerved in the memory of a ſucceſſion of admirers, and have had the good fortune to arrive at our times pure and uncorrupted.

DISSERTATION II.

ON THE TRAGIC BALLAD.

THAT species of poetry which we denominate Ballad, is peculiar to a barbarous period. In an advanced state of arts, the Comic Ballad assumes the form of the Song or Sonnet, and the Tragic or Heroic Ballad that of the higher Ode.

The cause of our pleasure in seeing a mournful event represented, or hearing it described, has been attempted to be explained by many critics *. It seems to arise from the mingled passions of Admiration of the art of the author, Curiosity to attend the termination, Delight arising from a reflection on our own security, and the Sympathetic Spirit.

* Aristotle, Scaliger, Dubos, Trapp in his Prælections, Hume, Essay on Tragedy; but, above all, Mr. Burke in his Enquiry into the Sublime and Beautiful.

In

In giving this pleasure, perhaps the Tragic Ballad yields to no effort of human genius. When we peruse a polished Tragedy or Ode, we admire the art of the author, and are led to praise the invention; but when we read an unartful description of a melancholy event, our passions are more intensely moved. The laboured productions of the informed composer resemble a Greek or Roman temple; when we enter it, we admire the art of the builder. The rude effusions of the Gothic Muse are like the monuments of their Architecture. We are filled with a religious reverence, and, forgetting our praise of the contriver, adore the present deity.

I believe no Tragic Ballad of renowned Antiquity has reached our times, if we deny the beautiful and pathetic CARMEN DE ATY in Catullus a title to this class; which, as a modern critic of note has observed *, seems a translation from some Greek *Dithyrambic* †, far more ancient than the times of that poet. His translation of Sappho's Ode might shew that he took a delight in the ancient Greek compositions, from which indeed he seems to have derived in a great measure his peculiarly delicate vein.

* Essay on the writings and genius of Pope, *p.* 324. 3*d ed.*

† The *Dithyrambics* were Heroic Songs, written with the highest glow of poetic fancy in honour of the ancient deities. Aristotle informs us, that the Greek Tragedy originated *from* them; as their Comedy did from their Pastoral Love Songs.

 But

But it was with the nations in a ſtate of barbarity that this effuſion of the heart flouriſhed as in it's proper ſoil; their ſocieties, rude and irregular, were full of viciſſitudes, and every hour ſubject to the moſt dreadful accidents. The Minſtrels, who only knew, and were inſpired by the preſent manners, caught the tale of mortality, and recorded it for the inſtruction and entertainment of others. It pleaſed by moving the paſſions, and, at the ſame time, afforded caution to their auditors to guard againſt ſimilar miſ-adventures.

It is amuſing to obſerve how expreſſive the poetry of every country is of its real manners. That of the Northern nations is ferocious to the higheſt degree. Nor need we wonder that thoſe, whoſe laws obliged them to decide the moſt trifling debate with the ſword *, delighted in a vein of poetry, which only painted deeds of blood, and objects horrible to the imagination. The ballad poetry of the Spaniards is tinged with the romantic gallantry of the nation. The hero is all complaiſance; and takes off his helmet in the heat of combat, when he thinks on his miſtreſs. That of the Engliſh is generous and brave. In their moſt noble ballad, Percy laments over the death of his

* Frotho etiam III. Danorum rex, quemadmodum Saxo, lib. V. refert, de qualibet controverſia ferre decerni ſanxit: ſpecioſius viribus quam verbis, confligendum exiſtimans. *Schedius de diis Ger. Syng.* II. *c.* 46.

mortal

mortal foe. That of the Scots is perhaps, like the face of their country, more various than the reſt. We find in it the bravery of the Engliſh, the gallantry of the Spaniſh, and I am afraid in ſome inſtances the ferocity of the Northern.

A late writer * has remarked, that, " the Scottiſh " tunes, whether melancholy or gay, whether amorous, " martial, or paſtoral, are in a ſtyle highly original, " and moſt feelingly expreſſive of all the paſſions from " the ſweeteſt to the moſt terrible." He proceeds, " Who was it that threw out thoſe dreadful wild ex- " preſſions of diſtraction and melancholy in *Lady Cul-* " *roſs's Dream?* an old compoſition, now I am afraid " loſt, perhaps becauſe it was almoſt too terrible for " the ear."

This compoſition is neither loſt, nor is it too terrible for the ear. On the contrary, a child might hear it repeated in a winter night without the ſmalleſt emotion. A copy † of it now lies before me, and as ſome curioſity

* Miſcellanies by John Armſtrong, M. D. vol. II. p. 254.

† It is intituled, " A Godly Dream compiled by Elizabeth " Melvil, Lady Culroſs younger, at the requeſt of a friend." Edinburgh, 1737, 12mo. p. 20. It is either reprinted from ſome former edition, or from a MS. It was written, I conjecture, about the end of the Sixteenth Century; but in this edition I ſuſpect ſeveral expreſſions are modernized and altered to accommodate it to the common capacity.

 The

curiosity may have been raised by the above remark, I shall here give an account of it. The dreadful and melancholy of this production are solely of the religious kind, and may have been deeply affecting to the enthusiastic at the period in which it was written: It begins thus;

Upon a day as I did mourn full sore,
For sundry things wherewith my soul was grieved,
My grief increased, and grew more and more,
I comfort fled, and could not be relieved;
With heaviness my heart was sore mischieved,
I loathed my life, I could not eat nor drink,
I might not speak, nor look to none that lived,
But mused alone, and diverse things did think.

This wretched world did so molest my mind,
I thought upon this false and iron age,
And how our hearts are so to vice inclined,
That Satan seems most fearfully to rage,
Nothing on earth my sorrow could aswage,
I felt my sin so strongly to increase;
I grieved the spirit was wont to be my pledge;
My soul was plunged into most deep distress.

The lady Culross here meant was Elizabeth daughter of Sir James Melvil of Halhill, and wife of John Colvil Commendator of Culross. She is believed to have been the mother of Samuel Colvil the satyrical poet, author of the Scots Hudibras, &c.

Her

Her Saviour is then ſuppoſed to appear in a dream, and lead her through many hair-breadth ſcapes into Heaven:

Through dreadful dens, which made my heart aghaſt,
He bare me up when I began to tire;
Sometimes we clamb oer cragie mountains high;
And ſometimes ſtayed on ugly braes of ſand,
They were ſo ſtay that wonder was to ſee;
But when I feared, he held me by the hand.—
Through great deſerts we wandered on our way.—
Forward we paſt on narrow bridge of tree,
Oer waters great which hideouſly did roar, &c.

The moſt terrible paſſage to a ſuperſtitious ear, is that in which ſhe ſuppoſes herſelf ſuſpended over the Gulph of Perdition:

Ere I was ware, one gripped me at laſt,
And held me high above a flaming fire.
The fire was great, the heat did pierce me ſore,
My faith grew weak, my grip was very ſmall.
I trembled faſt, my fear grew more and more.
My hands did ſhake that I held him withall,
At length they looſed, then I began to fall, &c.

At length ſhe arrives in view of the Heavenly manſions in a ſtanza, which, to alter a little her own expreſſion, 'Gliſters with *tinſel.*'

I looked up unto that caſtle fair
Gliſtering with gold; and ſhining ſilver bright
The ſtately towers did mount above the air;
They blinded me they caſt ſo great a light,
My heart was glad to ſee that joyful ſight,
My voyage then I thought it not in vain,
I him beſought to guide me there aright,
With many vows never to tire again.

And the whole concludes with an exhortation to a pious life.

But what has the Chriſtian religion to do with poetry? In the true poetic terrible, I believe, ſome paſſages in Hardyknute yield to no attempt of a ſtrong and dark fancy. The Ballad ſtyled Edward may, I fear, be rather adduced as an evidence that this diſpleaſes, when it riſes to a degree of the horrible, which that ſingular piece certainly partakes of.

The Pathetic is the other principal walk of the Tragic Muſe: and in this the Scotiſh Ballads yield to no compoſitions whatever. What can be imagined more moving than the cataſtrophes of Oſſian's Darthula, the moſt pathetic of all poems? or of Hardyknute,

nute, Child Maurice, and indeed most of the pieces now collected? Were ever the feelings of a fond mother expressed in a language equal in simplicity and pathos to that of lady Bothwell?—This leads me to remark, that the dialect in which the Scotish Ballads are written gives them a great advantage in point of touching the passions. Their language is rough and unpolished, and seems to flow immediately from the heart *. We meet with no concettos or far-fetched thoughts in them. They possess the pathetic power in the highest degree, because they do not affect it; and are striking, because they do not meditate to strike.

Most of the compositions now offered to the public, have already received approbation. The mutilated Fragment of Hardyknute formerly in print, was admired and celebrated by the best critics. As it is now, I am inclined to think, given in it's original perfection, it is certainly the most noble production in this style that ever appeared in the world. The manners and characters are strongly marked, and well preserved; the incidents deeply interesting; and the catastrophe new and affecting. I am indebted for most of the stanzas, now recovered, to the memory of a lady in Lanarkshire.

* Ὁ γὰρ ὄγκος δὲ τὸ ἐξ ἐπιτηδεύσεως ἅπαν ἀνθοποίητον.

Dionys. Hal.

A modern lyric poet of the first class * has pronounced Child Maurice a Divine Ballad. "Aristotle's "best rules," says he, "are observed in it in a manner that shews the author had never read Aristotle." Indeed if any one will peruse Aristotle's Art of Poetry with Dacier's Elucidations, and afterwards compare their most approved rules with this simple Ballad, he will find that they are better illustrated by this rude effort of the Gothic Muse, than by the most exquisite Tragedy of ancient or modern times. The Oedipus Tyrannus of Sophocles, the Athalie of Racine, the Merope of Maffei, and even the very excellent Drama, which seems immediately founded on it, not excepted; there being many delicate strokes in this original, which the plot adopted by that author forbade his making proper use of. This does honour at once to the unknown composer of this Ballad, and to the first of critics. In the former the reader will admire a genius, that, probably untracked by erudition, could produce a story corresponding to the intricate though natural rules of the Greek author. To the latter will be readily confirmed the applause of an ancient †, that, he was the secretary of Nature, and his pen was ever dipped in good sense.

* Mr. Gray. See his Letters published by Mr. Mason. Sect. IV. Let. XXV.

† Apud Suidam.

These,

These, and the other monuments of ancient Scotish Poetry, which have already appeared, are in this edition given much more correct; and a few are now first published from tradition. The Editor imagined they possessed some small beauties, else they would not have been added to this Selection. Their seeming antiquity was only regarded as it enhanced their real graces.

MDCCLXXVI *.

* These Dissertations, &c. were written of this date, but slight additions have been made to them from time to time; as the reader will observe from references to books published since that period.

HAVING

HAVING in the First of the foregoing Dissertations mentioned with applause the Spanish Ballads, or Romanzes, contained in the HISTORIA DE LAS GUERRAS CIVILES DE GRANADA, and that book being seldom to be met with, and written in a language of no wide study, the Editor has been induced to give a few translations from that work; the two which Dr. Percy has published having rather excited than gratified curiosity.

Before producing these translations, it may be proper to give some short account of the work whence they are taken. The History of the Civil Wars of Granada is a well-written narration of those dissentions which tore that kingdom in pieces, for some years before the period that Ferdinand and Isabella, king and queen of Christian Spain, conquered it, down to the time of conquest. The chief sources of those dissentions were the two great *Vandos*, or factions, of the Zegris and the Abencerrages; whose exploits and adventures, with those of their adherents, are here displayed with a minute detail that favours very strongly of romance, though the great outlines of the work are evidently founded on historical truth; which, if the reader

reader pleases, is indeed only another name for a certain species of romance.

This History, as we learn from the work itself towards the close, is a translation from the Arabic of an anonymous Moor, who fled to Africa with many of his countrymen, when Granada was yielded to the arms of Ferdinand. His grandson, by name Argutaafa, found this work among his grandfather's papers, and presented it to a Jew, called Rabbi Santo, who translated it into Hebrew; and gave the Arabic Original to Don Rodrigo Ponce de Leon, Conde de Baylen. That lord being interested by it, as his ancestors had been concerned in the wars there related, ordered the Jew to translate it into Castillan Spanish; and afterwards gave the translation to the Spanish editor, whose name from the first edition, Barcelona printed by Seb. Matevad, 1610, appears to be Ginez Perez.

On almost every occasion the author produces some romanze, as the voucher of his incidents, translations of a few of which shall now be produced. It must, however, be premised, that the first translation is merely meant to convey to the reader an idea of the verse in which most of the originals are written; for which purpose one of the feeblest was chosen, as, had strength of thought or incident been attempted in this way, the spirit would have totally evaporated in the midst of attention to the double rimes, of which the English language is remarkably penurious.

ROMANZE

ROMANZE I.

I.

AT the pleaſant dawn of morning,
  Mooriſh knights in numbers ſally,
To maintain a ſolemn turney
  In Granada's verdant valley.

II.

Juſting they wheel their fleet horſes;
  On his lance each warrior ſteady
Bears a rich and beauteous penon,
  Wrought with art by his fair lady.

III.

The bright ſun they dazzle, ſhewing
  Jupes of ſilk and golden tiſſue:
Each young hero hopes to ſoften
  His proud dame by that day's iſſue.

IV.

From the towers of proud Alhambra *
  Mooriſh ladies view the trial;
And among them two the faireſt
  Of the court without denial.

* *The celebrated palace of the Mooriſh kings of Granada.*

V.

Fatima they and Xarifa
 Love on both has play'd his quiver:
Thee, Xarifa, O that Alla
 Would from jealoufy deliver!

VI.

Tho friends they, for this has filence
 O'er them fpread his fullen pinion.
Fatima the heart has ftolen
 Of Xarifa's faithlefs minion.

VII.

Abendarrez call the rover;
 Guiltlefs fhe of his defection;
For of Fatima's firm paffion
 Abenamar was th' election.

VIII.

Spoke at length the wrong'd Xarifa,
 As with fcorn her rage to cover;
For fhe thought her friend with favour
 Heard the fuit of her falfe lover.

IX.

'Love cannot be hid, my fifter,
 'But himfelf he ftill difclofes;
'Of thy tongue where is the prattle?
 'Of thy checks where are the rofes?

X. 'Thou

X.

'Thou art not in love, I know it!
'See the cauſe of thy condition;
'Thy knight, Abendarrez, tilting,
'Hopes the prize with fond ambition.

XI.

Beauteous Fatima her ſilence
In wiſe anſwer thus has broken:
'Never yet did Love, Xarifa,
'Of my heart receive a token.

XII.

'If my ſpeech and colour leave me
'It is not without a reaſon;
'Short time ſince my gracious father
'Died by Alabez's treaſon.

XIII.

'And if ever Love, my ſiſter,
'To his law could bring me over,
'Abendarrez ſhould not win me,
'From thy charms a cruel rover.'

XIV.

Thus the Mooriſh dames have ſpoken;
Then in ſilence clos'd their prattle,
To remark each gallant chieftain
Who maintain'd the ſeeming battle.

ROMANZE II.

I.

WHEN valiant Ferdinand beheld
Granada to his proweſs yield;
And o'er Alhambra's higheſt tower
The banner fly of Chriſtian power;

II.

Thus to the flower of Spaniſh ground,
His peers and loyal leaders round,
The mandates of his mighty breaſt,
The monarch in his pride addreſs'd.

III.

'Who when the morning ſprings, will go
'Our chief againſt the mountain foe;
'And ſpread our princely enſign tall
'O'er Alpuxarra's rebel wall * ?

* *When Ferdinand was occupied with the acquiſition of Granada, Alpuxarra, and ſome other Mooriſh towns newly conquered, took the opportunity to revolt.*

IV. In

IV.

In ſilence every troubled peer
Read in each other's face his fear:
The journey full of perils great
They knew, and doubtful the retreat.

V.

Each tremulous beard in terror ſhook,
Till from his ſeat, with frowning look,
Alonſo de Aguilar ſprung
And thus beſpoke with fearleſs tongue.

VI.

'O king, for me is this emprize,
'And ſhame or praiſe that thence may riſe;
'The queen her ſovereign promiſe gave
'No other the bright claim ſhould have.'

VII.

With joy the king the valiant heard.
Soon as the morrow's dawn appear'd,
Alonſo with his eager van
To climb Nevada's heights began.

VIII.

Five hundred horſe to battle bred,
A thouſand infantry he led;
The Moors in ſilent ambuſh lay.
In crowds to guard the rocky way.

IX.

Amid the pathleſs cliffs the cry
Of conflict echoes to the ſky:
The cavalry no footing gain,
But fall by ſtony fragments ſlain.

X.

Alonſo, and the foot-array,
Sore leſſen'd by the bloody fray,
At length attain an upland dale,
Where countleſs Moors their ranks aſſail.

XI.

Tho bleed around whole bands of foes,
Yet who ſuch numbers may oppoſe?
The chief at length beheld his hoſt,
In one unbounded ſlaughter loſt.

XII.

Tho left alone, the lion-knight
Declines not the unequal fight;
Where'er he turns his eyes of fire,
As ſtruck by lightning crowds expire.

XIII.

Freſh Moors poſſeſs the bloody field;
No longer ſtrong his ſword to wield,
The victim of a thouſand wounds,
The ſhade of death the chief ſurrounds.

XIV. The

XIV.

Tho bravely dead, each coward Moor
With caitiff lance his body tore;
Then to Ogixar they him brought;
Where all to ſee the warrior fought.

XV.

Each Moor and Mooriſh dame with joy
Saw him, who wont their hopes deſtroy,
No more exert his matchleſs force,
But harmleſs ly a bleeding corſe.

XVI.

A Chriſtian captive of the crowd
Yet mov'd their tears with outcry loud:
For ſhe had nurs'd him at her breaſt,
And in the cradle ſooth'd his reſt.

XVII.

'Alonſo, Oh Alonſo brave!
'May heaven thy generous ſpirit have!
'The Moors of Alpuxara ſlew
'The braveſt knight that fame e'er knew.'

ROMANZE III.

I.

EIGHT to eight, and ten to ten,
  Knights of valour and renown,
Turney in Toledo fair
  The glad day of peace to crown.

II.

An high feſtival the king
  Gives his pleaſure to evince;
Concord reigns between his brother
  And Granada's warlike prince.

III.

Others ſay the feaſt is given
  Zelindaxa bright to pleaſe;
Miſtreſs of the king's affection,
  She ordains him pain or eaſe.

IV.

The Zarrazins and Aliatores,
  There in gallant union ride;
The Alariſés and Azarqués
  Them oppoſe with equal pride.

V. The

V.

The Zarrazins, a noble band,
On ſorrel horſes there were ſeen;
Their mantles and their jupes diſtinguiſh'd
By the orange hue and green.

VI.

On their ſhields a cimiter,
Bent as Cupid's bow, they wore;
And the words FUEGO Y SANGRE*,
As the choſen motto bore.

VII.

Equals in the gallant ſhow
Next the Aliatores ſhone;
In carnation garbs array'd
With white foliages beſtrown.

VIII.

For device, upon the ſtrength
Of Atlas ſtood a ſtable heaven;
TENDRELO HASTA QUE CANSE †
For the motto there was given.

* *Fire and blood.*

† *He will ſupport it till he is weary.*

IX.

Them enſued the Alariſés
In moſt coſtly manner clad;
Their ſleeves right curiouſly were purfled
On the yellow cloth and red.

X.

A naked Hercules they gave,
Who a ſavage monſter tore;
And above FUERCAS VALEN *
As the valiant word they wore.

XI.

Them the eight Azarqués follow'd,
And in pride exceeded all;
Straw's pale dye and browniſh gray
Were their hues of feſtival.

XII.

On each chieftain's verdant ſhield
Held two daring hands a ſphere;
EN LO VERDE TODO CABE †
As the words of honour were.

* *Strength is powerful.*

† *In the green every thing is comprehended.*

XIII. Among

XIII.

Among this band the king beheld
  The rival of his lady's love,
And jealousy his cruel heart
  To thoughts of utmost fury drove.

XIV.

To Selin thus, high constable,
  The sovereign spoke in frantic mood:
' The sun that dazzles now mine eyes,
  ' Ere long I trust shall set in blood.'

XV.

The graceful knight so strongly threw *
  His rods, they vanish'd in the air;
Nor could the power of keenest eye,
  Their progress or their fall declare.

XVI.

Each lady, from the windows high,
  Or scaffolds, that enjoy'd the sight,
With anxious looks of fond desire
  Bent forwards to behold the knight.

* *It was anciently the custom for the Spanish gentry to amuse themselves while on horseback with throwing small rods, or canes, into the air; on darting of which with such force and skill as to delude the eye, they much valued themselves.*

XVII.

As he advances or retires,
 ' May heaven thee ſave!' the vulgar cry:
While, burnt with jealouſy's fierce flames,
 The king ſtill anſwers, ' Let him die!'

XVIII.

Bold Zelindaxa, ſovereign fair,
 As near the royal tower he drew,
Tho ' Hold! hold!' cried the angry king,
 Sprinkled the chief with fragrant dew.

XIX.

The turney ſtopp'd: in ſilence deep,
 And expectation, ſtood the ring;
While, giving reaſon's rein to rage,
 ' Arreſt the traitor!' cried the king.

XX.

The two firſt troops their lances ſeize
 The princely mandate to fulfill.
Alas! what barrier can be ſet
 Againſt an amorous monarch's will!

XXI.

The other two defence prepar'd,
 Had not the Azarqué to them ſaid,
' Friends, tho the king's love has no laws,
 ' Remember laws for your's were made.

XXII. ' Lower

XXII.

'Lower your lances, tho my foes
'Are eager fee my blood to fpill.
'Alas, what barrier can be fet
'Againft an amorous monarch's will!

XXIII.

They took the noble Moor. His friends
Drop'd tears of rage his fate to fee.
In wild diforder rufh'd the croud,
By force the captive knight to free.

XXIV.

They had no chief to guide their ire,
And fled before fuperior fkill.
Alas, what barrier can be fet,
Againft an amorous monarch's will!

XXV.

Fair Zelindaxa cried aloud,
'Refcue, ye Moors, your warrior brave!'
And rofe as if fhe meant to leap
From the high tower her knight to fave.

XXVI.

Her mother her embrac'd, and cried,
'Ah, are you mad yourfelf to kill!
'Alas, what barrier can be fet
'Againft an amorous monarch's will!'

XXVII. The

XXVII.

The furious king a meſſage ſent
  The mournful damſel to convey
To a lone manſion of her friends,
  In laſting durance there to ſtay.

XXVIII.

'Tell him,' ſhe ſaid, 'where'er I go,
  'My firm love ſhall attend me ſtill.
'Alas, what barrier can be ſet
  'Againſt an amorous monarch's will!'

ROMANZE IV*.

I.

ALONG San Lucar's ample ſquare
  See gallant Gazul ride;
In ſnowey hue array'd, and green,
  And purple's radiant pride.
To Gelves he deſigns to go,
  His valiant ſkill to try;
In turnament with many a knight
  Of high renown to vie.

II.

The chief a noble dame adores;
  Of her farewell to take,
A thouſand anxious turns before
  Yon manſion fee him make.
Lo, from the balcony at length,
  The lovely maid inclines,
As o'er a diſtant hill the morn,
  In roſy radiance ſhines.

* *This ballad is compoſed of three different ones on the ſame ſubject; the firſt beginning,* Por la plaça de San Lucar; *the ſecond,* Sale la eſtrella de Venus; *and the third,* No de tal braveza lleno.

III. Swift

III.

Swift from his ſteed the warrior lights,
And kneels upon the ground,
As ſtruck with awe: ſuch power has love
The valiant to confound.
'O fair,' he cries with trembling voice,
'This day muſt fame be mine:
'What chance can hurt me now that I
'Have ſeen thy charms divine?

IV.

'Yet of thy favour I beſeech
'Some badge to bear along *;
'That, with it grac'd, my haughty lance
'May as my love be ſtrong.'
In jealous rage the maid replied,
For then full well ſhe knew
That Zaida, his firſt deſire,
An elder duty drew.

V.

'If in the combat thy ſucceſs
'My heart's deſire may crown;
'No more, falſe knight, ſhalt thou return,
'But life loſe, and renown.

* *It was the cuſtom for ladies to preſent their lovers with the penon or ſtreamer they were to wear on their lance in combat or turney. The penon was commonly richly inwoven with the lady's cypher.* See Stanza XIII.

'To God I speak my eager wish,
'Sincere as thou dost lye,
'That in the fight by secret foes
'Ignobly thou mayst die.

VI.

'O may thy enemies be strong!
'Thy friends all dastards prove!
'O be thou dead, as is thy fame,
'And not even pity move!'
The leader thinks she speaks in jest,
And thus in haste replies;
'The Moor who would us set at strife,
'Believe me, lady, lies.

VII.

'May all thy curses on him light!
'My soul must now abhor
'That Zaida; tho wont, I own,
Her beauty to adore.
'After long years of service, she
'For a base Moor me left—'
The fair retired, nor more would hear,
Of patience quite bereft.

VIII.

A page appear'd, and gallant ſteeds
  Him brought in rich array:
'Return,' the frantic warrior cried,
  'We try no arms this day.'
In frenzy then againſt the wall
  That hid his fair from view,
So ſierce he tilted, that his ſpear
  In thouſand ſplinters flew.

IX.

In anguiſh now he paus'd a while,
  Now rode in furious mood,
Till madneſs fired his inmoſt ſoul,
  And prompted deeds of blood.
His wandering way to Xerez far
  Along the ſhore he held;
Where with her ſire his former love,
  Falſe Zaida, now dwell'd.

X.

The ſtar of eve with golden light
  Illumed the weſtern wave,
When near to Xerez Gazul drew,
  As Rodamonte brave.

Not

Not he, that king of Argel high,
 When for his fair he ſtrove
With Mandricardo, ſtood in praiſe
 Young Gazul's name above.

XI.

Now near her manſion, with freſh rage
 His dauntleſs boſom burn'd;
And thus he ſpoke, while plaintive waves
 And rocks the ſound return'd.
'O Zaida, more faithleſs far
 'Than that inconſtant ſea;
'Not half ſo ſavage are theſe rocks,
 'Not half ſo hard as thee!

XII.

'How can'ſt thou give thy youthful hand
 'To him thy ſuitor old;
'And leave the riches of the mind
 'For ſordid wealth of gold?
'Oh, may ev'n he, thy ſuitor old,
 'Thy falſhood learn to ſcorn!
'May never love thy anxious nights,
 'Nor joy thy days adorn.

XIII.

‘ At zambra *, nor at feſtival,
‘ May never knight appear,
‘ Thy cypher on embroider’d ſleeve,
‘ Or ſilken badge to bear.
‘ May jealouſy ev’n of his age
‘ Thy peace ſtill violate.
‘ May he live long ! Thy fierceſt foe
‘ Can wiſh no worſe a fate.’

XIV.

Thus as he ſpoke the gradual night
Deſcended all around ;
And, as he near the manſion drew,
Of mirth he heard the ſound.
Sudden before a ruſhing croud
The doors were open thrown ;
And thro’ the gloom in bright array
A thouſand torches ſhone.

XV.

In midſt the future huſband held
Young Zaida’s falſe hand.
To church they went, where ſtood the prieſt
To fix the ſacred band.

* *A moreſque dance.*

This

This cruel ſight when Gazul ſaw,
His madneſs found new flame;
A while he reſted, till at hand
The brilliant troop now came.

XVI.

Then ſpurr'd his ſteed into the midſt,
And thus his lady's choice
Addreſs'd, while all in ſudden fear
Stood trembling at his voice.
'Hope not, baſe traitor, to enjoy
'This lady, once my love;
'Defend thyſelf if e'er thy arm
'Could ſkill or valour prove.

XVII.

He ſpoke. They fought. The aged Moor
Lay dead upon the ground.
Swift to revenge his wretched fall,
His numerous friends drew round.
Againſt their force the warrior ſtood
With more than mortal might:
Then, ſlow retreating, refuge found
Amid the ſhades of night.

La plupart de ces chansons sont de vieilles romances dont les airs ne sont pas piquans; mais ils ont je ne sais quoi d'antique et de doux qui touche a la longue.

Rousseau.

HARDYKNUTE.

AN HEROIC BALLAD.

PART I.

STATELY ſtept he eaſt the ha,
  And ſtately ſtept he weſt;
Full ſeventy yeirs he now had ſene,
  With ſcerce ſevin yeirs of reſt.
He livit whan Britons breach of faith
  Wrocht Scotland meikle wae,
And ay his ſword tauld to their coſt
  He was their deidly fae.

Hie on a hill his caſtle ſtude,
  With halls and touris a hicht,
And gudely chambers fair to ſee,
  Whar he lodgit mony a knicht.
His dame ſa peirles anes, and fair,
  For chaſte, and bewtie, ſene,
Na marrow had in a the land,
  Save Emergard the quene.

Full thirtein ſons to him ſhe bare,
All men of valour ſtout,
In bluidy ficht, with ſword in hand,
Nyne loſt their lives bot doubt;
Four yit remaind; lang mote they live
To ſtand by liege and land:
Hie was their fame, hie was their micht,
And hie was their command.

Greit luve they bare to Fairly fair,
Their ſiſter ſaft and deir,
Her girdle ſhawd her middle jimp,
And gowdin gliſt her hair.
What waefou wae her bewtie bred!
Waefou to young and auld,
Waefou I trow to kyth and kin,
As ſtory ever tauld.

The king of Norſe, in ſummer tide,
Puft up with pouir and micht,
Landed in fair Scotland the yle,
Wi mony a hardie knicht.
The tidings to our gude Scots king
Came as he ſat at dyne
With noble chiefs in braive aray,
Drinking the bluid red wyne.

" To horſe, to horſe, my royal liege!
" Your faes ſtand on the ſtrand;
" Full twenty thouſand glittering ſpeirs
" The cheifs of Norſe command.
" Bring me my ſteid Mage dapple gray."
Our gude king raiſe and cryd:
A truſtier beiſt in all the land,
A Scots king nevir ſeyd.

" Gae, little page, tell Hardyknute,
" Wha lives on hill ſa hie,
" To draw his ſword, the dreid of faes,
" And haſte and follow me."
The little page flew ſwift as dart,
Flung by his maſter's arm;
' Cum down, cum down, lord Hardyknute,
' And red your king frae harm.'

Then reid, reid grew his dark-brown cheiks
Sae did his dark-brown brow;
His luiks grew kene, as they were wont
In danger grit to do.
He has tane a horn as grene as graſs,
And gien five ſounds ſa ſhrill,
That tries in grene wode ſhuke thereat,
Sae loud rang ilka hill.

His ſons in manly ſport and glie
  Had paſt the ſummer's morn ;
Whan lo ! down in a graſſy dale,
  They heard their father's horn.
' That horn, quoth they, neir ſounds in peace,
  ' We have other ſport to bide ;'
And ſune they hied them up the hill,
  And ſune were at his ſide.

" Late, late yeſtrene, I weind in peace ,
  " To end my lengthend lyfe ;
" My age micht well excuſe my arm
  " Frae manly feats of ſtryfe :
" But now that Norſe does proudly boaſt
  " Fair Scotland to enthral,
" It's neir be ſaid of Hardyknute,
  " He feird to fecht or fall.

" Robin of Rothſay bend thy bow,
  " Thy arrows ſhute ſa leil,
" That mony a comely countenance
  " They've turn'd to deidly pale.
" Braive Thomas taike ye but your lance,
  " Ye neid na weapons mair ;
" Gif ye fecht wi't, as ye did anes,
  " Gainſt Weſtmoreland's ferce heir.

" And

"And Malcolm, licht of fute as ſtag
"That runs in foreſt wilde,
"Get me my thouſands thrie of men
"Weil bred to ſword and ſhield:
"Bring me my horſe and harniſine,
"My blade of metal clere."
If faes but kend the hand it bare,
They ſune had fled for feir.

"Farewil my dame ſae peirleſs gude,"
And tuke her by the hand,
"Fairer to me in age you ſeim
"Than maids for bewtie famd:
"My youngeſt ſon ſall here remain,
"To guard theſe ſtately touirs,
"And ſhute the ſilver bolt that keips
"Sae faſt your painted bowers."

And firſt ſhe wet her comely cheiks,
And then her boddice grene;
The ſilken cords of twirtle twiſt
Were plet with ſilver ſhene;
And apron ſet with mony a dyce
Of neidle-wark ſae rare,
Wove by nae hand, as ye may gueſs,
Save that of Fairly fair.

And he has ridden our muir and moſs,
  Our hills and mony a glen,
When he cam to a wounded knicht,
  Making a heavy mane:
‘ Here maun I lye, here maun I dye
  ‘ By treacheries fauſe gyles;
‘ Witleſs I was that eir gave faith
  ‘ To wicked woman's ſmyles.’

“ Sir knicht, gin ye were in my bouir,
  “ To lean on ſilken ſeat,
“ My lady's kindlie care you'd pruve
  “ Wha neir kend deidly hate;
“ Hirſell wald watch ye all the day,
  “ Hir maids at deid of nicht;
“ And Fairly fair your heart would cheir,
  “ As ſhe ſtands in your ſicht.

“ Ariſe young knicht, and mount your ſteid,
  “ Bricht lows the ſhynand day;
“ Chuſe frae my menie wham ye pleiſe,
  “ To leid ye on the way.”
Wi ſmyleſs luik, and viſage wan
  The wounded knicht replyd,
‘ Kind chieftain your intent purſue,
  ‘ For heir I maun abide.

'To me nae after day nor nicht
'Can eir be ſweit or fair;
'But ſune benethe ſum draping trie,
'Cauld dethe ſall end my care.'
Still him to win ſtrave Hardyknute,
Nor ſtrave he lang in vain;
Short pleiding eithly micht prevale,
Him to his lure to gain.

"I will return wi ſpeid to bide,
"Your plaint and mend your wae:
"But private grudge maun neir be quelled,
"Before our countries fae.
"Mordac, thy eild may beſt be ſpaird
"The fields of ſtryfe fraemang;
"Convey Sir knicht to my abode,
"And meiſe his egre pang."

Syne he has gane far hynd, out owr
Lord Chattan's land ſae wyde;
That lord a worthy wicht was ay,
Whan faes his courage ſeyd:
Of Pictiſh race, by mother's ſide:
Whan Picts ruled Caledon,
Lord Chattan claim'd the princely maid
When he ſav'd Pictiſh crown.

Now with his ferce and ſtalwart train
He recht a riſing hicht,
Whar brad encampit on the dale,
Norſe army lay in ſicht;
"Yonder my valiant ſons, full ferce
"Our raging rievers wait,
"On the unconquerit Scottiſh ſwaird
"To try with us their fate.

"Mak oriſons to him that ſav'd
"Our ſauls upon the rude;
"Syne braively ſhaw your veins are filld
"Wi Caledonian bluid."
Then furth he drew his truſtie glaive,
While thouſands all around,
Drawn frae their ſheiths glanc'd in the ſun,
And loud the bugils ſound.

To join his king, adown the hill
In haſte his march he made,
While playand pibrochs minſtrals meit
Afore him ſtately ſtrade.
'Thriſe welcum, valiant ſtoup of weir,
'Thy nation's ſheild and pride,
'Thy king na reaſoun has to feir,
'Whan thou art by his ſide.

Whan

Whan bows were bent, and darts were thrawn,
For thrang ſcerce cold they flie,
The darts clave arrows as they met,
Eir faes their dint mote drie.
Lang did they rage, and fecht full ferce,
Wi little ſkaith to man;
But bluidy, bluidy was the feild
Or that lang day was done!

The king of Scots that ſindle bruik'd
The war that luik'd like play,
Drew his braid ſword, and brake his bow,
Sen bows ſeim'd but delay.
Quoth noble Rothſay, 'Mine I'll keep,
'I wate it's bleid a ſcore.'
"Haſte up my merrie men," cry'd the king,
As he rade on before.

The king of Norſe he ſocht to find,
Wi him to menſe the faucht;
But on his forehead there did licht
A ſharp unſonſie ſhaft:
As he his hand pat up to feil
The wound, an arrow kein,
O waefu chance! there pind his hand
In midſt atweene his eyne.

'Revenge!

'Revenge! revenge!' cryd Rothsay's heir,
'Your mail-coat sall nocht bide
'The strenth and sharpness of my dart,'
Whilk shared the reiver's side.
Anither arrow weil he mark'd
It perc'd his neck in twa;
His hands then quat the silver reins,
He law as eard did fa.

'Sair bleids my liege! Sair, sair he bleids!
Again with micht he drew,
And gesture dreid his sturdy bow;
Fast the braid arrow flew:
Wa to the knicht he ettled at;
Lament now quene Elgreid;
Hire dames to wail your darling's fall,
His youth, and comely meid.

'Tak aff, tak aff his costly jupe,'
(Of gold well was it twin'd,
Knit like the fowler's net, throuch whilk
His steily harnes shynd.)
'Beir Norse that gift frae me, and bid
'Him venge the bluid it weirs;
'Say if he face my bended bow
'He sure nae weapon feirs.'

Proud

Proud Norse with giant body tall,
  Braid shoulder, and arms strong;
Cryd, 'Whar is Hardyknute sae famd,
  'And feird at Britain's throne?
'Tho Britons tremble at his name,
  'I sune sall mak him wail,
'That eir my sword was made sae sharp,
  'Sae saft his coat of mail.

That brag his stout heart could na bide,
  It lent him youthfu micht:
"I'm Hardyknute. This day," he cryed,
  "To Scotland's king I hicht
"To lay thee law as horse's hufe;
  "My word I mean to keip!"
Syne with the first dint eir he strake
  He gar'd his body bleid.

Norse ene like grey gosehauk staird wilde,
  He sich'd wi shame and spyte;
'Disgrac'd is now my far famd arm
  'That left thee pouir to stryke.'
Syne gied his helm a blow sae fell,
  It made him down to stoup,
Sae law as he to ladies us'd,
  In courtly gyse to lout.

Full

Full ſune he rais'd his bent body;
  His bou he marveld ſair,
Sen blaws till than on him but dar'd
  As touch of Fairly fair.
Noiſe ferlied too as ſair as he,
  To ſee his ſtately luik;
Sae ſune as eir he ſtrake a fae,
  Sae ſune his lyfe he tuke.

Whar, like a fyre to hether ſet,
  Bauld Thomas did advance,
A ſturdy fae, with luik enrag'd,
  Up towards him did prance.
He ſpurd his ſteid throuch thickeſt ranks
  The hardy youth to quell;
Wha ſtude unmuvit at his approach
  His furie to repell.

' That ſhort brown ſhaft, ſae meinly trimd,
  ' Lukes like poor Scotland's geir;
' But dreadfu ſeims the ruſty point!'
  And loud he leuch in jeir.
" Aft Britons blude has dim'd its ſhyne
  " It's point cut ſhort their vaunt."
Syne perc'd the boſter's bairded cheik
  Nae time he tuke to taunt.

Short while he in his ſadil ſwang;
  His ſtirrip was nae ſtay,
But feible hang his unbent knie,
  Sair taken he was, fey!
Swyth on the harden'd clay he fell,
  Richt far was heard the thud;
But Thomas luk'd not as he lay
  All waltering in his blude.

Wi careles geſture, mind unmuv'd,
  On rade he north the plain
His ſeim in peace, or ferceſt ſtryſe,
  Ay reckleſs, and the ſame.
Nor yit his heart dames' dimpeld cheik
  Cold meiſe ſaft luve to bruik;
Till vengefu Ann returnd his ſcorn,
  Then languid grew his luke.

In thrauis of dethe, wi wallow'd cheik,
  All panting on the plain,
The bleiding corps of warriours lay,
  Neir to ariſe again:
Neir to return to native land;
  Na mair wi blythſum ſounds
To boaſt the glories of that day,
  And ſhaw their ſhynand wounds.

There

There on a lee, whar ſtands a croſs
Set up for monument,
Thouſands fu ferce, that ſummer's day,
Fill'd kene wars black intent.
Let Scots while Scots praiſe Hardyknute
Let Norſe the name aye dreid;
Ay how he faucht, aft how he ſpaird,
Sall lateſt ages reid.

On Norway's coaſt the widow'd dame
May waſh the rocks wi teirs,
May lang luke owr the ſhiples ſeas
Before her mate appeirs.
Ceiſe, Emma, ceiſe to hope in vain,
Thy lord lyes in the clay;
The valiant Scots na rievers thole
To carry lyfe away.

Loud and chill blew the weſtlin wind,
Sair beat the heavy ſhouir,
Mirk grew the nicht ere Hardyknute
Wan neir his ſtately touir:
His touir that us'd wi torches bleiſe
To ſhyne ſae far at nicht
Seim'd now as black as mourning weid:
Na marvel ſair he ſich'd.

"There's

"There's na licht in my lady's bouir,
"There's na licht in my ha;
"Na blynk shynes round my Fairly fair,
"Na ward stands on my wa.
"What bodes it? Robert, Thomas, say."
Na answer fits their dreid.
"Stand back my sons I'll be your gyde."
But by they past wi speid.

"As fast I ha sped owr Scotland's faes—"
There ceis'd his brag of weir,
Sair shamd to mind ocht but his dame,
And maiden Fairly fair.
Black feir he felt, but what to feir
He wist nae yit wi dreid:
Sair shuke his body, sair his limbs
And a the warriour flied.

PART II.

" RETURN, return, ye men of bluid,
  " And bring me back my chylde!"
A dolefu voice frae mid the ha
  Reculd, wi echoes wylde.
Bestraught wi dule and dreid, na pouir
  Had Hardyknute at a;
Full thrise he raught his ported speir,
  And thrise he let it fa.

" O haly God, for his deir sake,
  " Wha savd us on the rude——
He tint his praier, and drew his glaive,
  Yet reid wi Norland bluid.
" Brayd on, brayd on, my stalwart sons,
  " Grit cause we ha to feir;
" But ay the canny ferce contemn
  " The hap they canna veir."

' Return, return, ye men of bluid,
  ' And bring me back my chylde!'
The dolefu voice frae mid the ha
  Reculd, wi echoes wylde.
The storm grew rife, throuch a the lift
  The rattling thunder rang,
The black rain shour'd, and lichtning glent
  Their harnisine alang.

What

What feir poſſeſt their boding breeſts
 Whan, by the gloomy glour,
The caſtle ditch wi deed bodies
 They ſaw was filled out owr!
Quoth Hardyknute " I wold to Chryſte
 " The Norſe had wan the day,
" Sae I had keipt at hame but anes,
 " Thilk bluidy feats to ſtay."

Wi ſpeed they paſt, and ſyne they recht
 The baſe-courts ſounding bound,
Deip groans ſith heard, and throuch the mirk
 Lukd wiſtfully around.
The moon, frae hind a ſable cloud,
 Wi ſudden twinkle ſhane,
Whan, on the cauldrif eard, they fand
 The gude Sir Mordac layn.

Beſprent wi gore, fra helm to ſpur,
 Was the trew-heartit knicht;
Swith frae his ſteid ſprang Hardyknute
 Muv'd wi the heavy ſicht.
" O ſay thy maſter's ſhield in weir,
 " His ſawman in the ha,
" What hatefu chance cold ha the pouir
 To lay thy eild ſae law?"

To his complaint the bleiding knicht
  Returnd a piteous mane,
And recht his hand, whilk Hardyknute
  Claucht ſtreitly in his ain:
'Gin eir ye ſee lord Hardyknute,
  'Frae Mordac ye maun ſay,
'Lord Draffan's treaſoun to confute
  'He uſd his ſteddieſt fay.'

He micht na mair, for cruel dethe
  Forbad him to proceid;
"I vow to God, I winna ſleip
  "Till I ſee Draffan bleid.
"My ſons your ſiſter was owr fair:
  "But bruik he ſall na lang
"His gude betide; my laſt forbode
  "He'll trow belyve na ſang.

"Bown ye my eydent friends to kyth
  "To me your luve ſae deir;
"The Norſe' defeat mote weil perſuade
  "Nae riever ye neid feir."
The ſpeirmen wi a michty ſhout,
  Cryd 'Save our maſter deir!
'While he dow beir the ſway bot care
  'Nae reiver we ſall feir.'

'Return,

'Return, return, ye men of bluid
  'And bring me back my chylde!'
The dolefu voice frae mid the ha
  Reculd wi echoes wylde.
"I am to wyte my valiant friends:"
  And to the ha they ran,
The ſtately dore full ſtreitly ſteiked
  Wi iron boltis thrie they fand.

The ſtately dore, thouch ſtreitly ſteiked
  Wi waddin iron boltis thrie,
Richt ſune his micht can eithly gar
  Frae aff it's hinges flie.
"Whar ha ye tane my dochter deir?
  "Mair wold I ſee her deid
"Than ſee her in your bridal bed
  "For a your portly meid.

"What thouch my gude and valiant lord
  "Lye ſtrecht on the cauld clay?
"My ſons the dethe may ablins ſpair
  "To wreak their ſiſters wae."
Sae did ſhe crune wi heavy cheir,
  Hyt luiks, and bleirit eyne;
Then teirs firſt wet his manly cheik
  And ſnawy baird bedeene.

‘ Na riever here, my dame ſae deir,
  ‘ But your leil lord you ſee;
‘ May hieſt harm betide his life
  ‘ Wha brocht ſic harm to thee!
‘ Gin anes ye may beleive my word,
  ‘ Nor am I uſd to lie,
‘ By day-prime he or Hardyknute
  ‘ The bluidy dethe ſhall die.’

The ha, whar late the linkis bricht
  Sae gladſum ſhind at een,
Whar penants gleit a gowden bleiſe
  Our knichts and ladys ſhene,
Was now ſae mirk, that, throuch the bound,
  Nocht mote they wein to ſee,
Alſe throuch the ſouthern port the moon
  Let fa a blinkand glie.

“ Are ye in ſuith my deir luvd lord?”
  Nae mair ſhe doucht to ſay,
But ſwounit on his harneſt neck
  Wi joy and tender fay.
To ſee her in ſic baleſu ſort
  Revived his ſelcouth feirs;
But ſune ſhe raiſd her comely luik,
  And ſaw his faing teirs.

" Ye are nae wont to greit wi wreuch,
" Grit cause ye ha I dreid;
" Hae a our sons their lives redemd
" Frae furth the dowie feid?"
' Saif are our valiant sons, ye see,
' But lack their sister deir;
' When she's awa, bot any doubt,
' We ha grit cause to feir.'

" Of a our wrangs, and her depart,
" Whan ye the suith sall heir,
" Na marvel that ye ha mair cause,
" Than ye yit weit, to feir.
" O wharefore heir yon feignand knicht
" Wi Mordac did ye send?
" Ye suner wald ha perced his heart
" Had ye his ettling kend."

' What may ye mein my peirles dame?
' That knicht did muve my ruthe
' We balefu mane; I did na dout
' His curtesie and truthe.
' He maun ha tint wi sma renown
' His life in this fell rief;
' Richt sair it grieves me that he heir
' Met sic an ill relief.'

Quoth ſhe, wi teirs that down her cheiks
  Ran like a ſilver ſhouir,
" May ill befa the tide that brocht
  " That fauſe knicht to our touir:
" Ken'd ye na Draffan's lordly port,
  " Thouch cled in knichtly graith?
" Tho hidden was his hautie luik
  " The viſor black benethe?"

' Now, as I am a knicht of weir,
  ' I thocht his ſeeming trew;
' But, that he ſae deceived my ruthe,
  ' Full ſairly he ſall rue.'
" Sir Mordac to the ſounding ha
  " Came wi his cative fere;"
' My ſire has ſent this wounded knicht
  ' To pruve your kyndlie care.

' Your ſell maun watch him a the day,
  ' Your maids at deid of nicht;
' And Fairly fair his heart maun cheir
  ' As ſhe ſtands in his ſicht.'
" Nae ſuner was Sir Mordac gane,
  " Than up the featour ſprang;"
' The luve alſe o your dochter deir
  ' I feil na ither pang.

‘ Tho Hardyknute lord Draffan's ſuit
‘ Refus'd wi mickle pryde ;
‘ By his gude dame and Fairly fair
‘ Let him not be deny'd.'
“ Nocht muvit wi the cative's ſpeech,
“ Nor wi his ſtern command ;
“ I treaſoun ! cryd, and Kenneth's blade
“ Was gliſterand in his hand.

“ My ſon lord Draffan heir you ſee,
“ Wha means your ſiſter's fay
“ To win by guile, when Hardyknute
“ Strives in the irie fray.”
‘ Turn thee ! thou riever Baron, turn !'
“ Bauld Kenneth cryd aloud ;
“ But, ſune as Draffan ſpent his glaive,
“ My ſon lay in his bluid.”

‘ I did nocht grein that bluming face
‘ That dethe ſae ſune ſold pale ;
‘ Far leſs that my trew luve, throuch me,
‘ Her brither's dethe ſold wail.
‘ But ſyne ye ſey our force to prive,
‘ Our force we ſall you ſhaw !'
“ Syne the ſhrill-ſounding horn bedeen
“ He tuik frae down the wa.

"Ere the portculie could be flung,
"His kyth the base-court fand;
"When scantly o their count a teind
"Their entrie micht gainstand.
"Richt sune the raging rievers stude
"At their fause master's syde,
"Wha, by the haly maiden, sware
"Na harm sold us betide.

"What syne befell ye weil may guess,
"Reft o our eilds delicht."
'We sall na lang be reft, by morne
'Sall Fairly glad your sicht.
'Let us be gane, my sons, or now
'Our meny chide our stay;
'Fareweil my dame; your dochter's luve
'Will sune cheir your effray.'

Then pale pale grew her teirfu cheik;
"Let ane o my sons thrie
"Alane gyde this emprize, your eild
"May ill sic travel drie.
"O whar were I, were my deir lord,
"And a my sons, to bleid!
"Better to bruik the wrang than sae
"To wreak the hie misdede."

The

The gallant Rothſay roſe bedeen
His richt of age to pleid;
And Thomas ſhawd his ſtrenthy ſpeir;
And Malcolm mein'd his ſpeid.
' My ſons your ſtryfe I gladly ſee,
' But it ſall neir be ſayne,
' That Hardyknute ſat in his ha,
' And heird his ſon was ſlayne.

' My lady deir, ye neid na feir;
' The richt is on our ſyde:'
Syne riſing with richt frawart haſte
Nae parly wald he byde.
The lady ſat in heavy mude,
Their tuneſu march to heir,
While, far ayont her ken, the ſound
Na mair mote roun her eir.

O ha ye ſein ſum glitterand touir,
Wi mirrie archers crownd,
Wha vaunt to ſee their trembling fae
Keipt frae their countrie's bound?
Sic auſum ſtrenth ſhawd Hardyknute;
Sic ſeimd his ſtately meid;
Sic pryde he to his meny bald,
Sic feir his faes he gied,

Wi glie they paſt our mountains rude,
Owr muirs and moſſes weit;
Sune as they ſaw the riſing ſun,
On Draffan's touirs it gleit.
O Fairly bricht I marvel ſair
That featour eer ye lued,
Whaſe treaſoun wrocht your father's bale,
And ſhed your brither's blude!

The ward ran to his youthfu lord,
Wha ſleipd his bouir intill:
'Nae time for ſleuth, your raging faes
'Fare doun the weſtlin hill.
'And, by the libbard's gowden low
'In his blue banner braid,
'That Hardyknute his dochtir ſeiks,
'And Draffans dethe, I rede.'

"Say to my bands of matchleſs micht,
"Wha camp law in the dale,
"To buſk their arrows for the fecht,
"And ſtreitly gird their mail.
"Syne meit me here, and wein to find
"Nae juſt or turney play;
"Whan Hardyknute braids to the field,
"War bruiks na lang delay."

His

His halbrik bricht he brac'd bedeen;
Fra ilka ſkaith and harm
Securit by a warloc auld,
Wi mony a fairy charm.
A ſeimly knicht cam to the ha:
' Lord Draffan I thee braive,
' Frae Hardyknute my worthy lord,
' To fecht wi ſpeir or glaive.'

" Your hautie lord me braives in vain
" Alane his micht to prive,
" For wha, in ſingle feat of weir,
" Wi Hardyknute may ſtrive?
" But ſith he meins our ſtrenth to ſey,
" On caſe he ſune will find,
" That thouch his bands leave mine in ire,
" In force they're far behind.

" Yet cold I wete that he wald yield
" To what bruiks nae remeid,
" I for his dochter wald nae hain
" To ae half o my ſteid."
Sad Hardyknute apart frae a
Leand on his birniſt ſpeir;
And, whan he on his Fairly deimd,
He ſpar'd nae ſich nor teir.

" What

" What meins the felon cative vile?
  " Bruiks this reif na remeid?
" I scorn his gylefu vows ein thouch
  " They recht to a his steid."
Bownd was lord Draffan for the fecht,
  Whan lo! his Fairly deir
Ran frae her hie bouir to the ha
  Wi a the speid of feir.

Ein as the rudie star of morne
  Peirs throuch a cloud of dew,
Sae did she seim, as round his neck
  Her snawy arms she threw.
' O why, O why, did Fairly wair
  ' On thee her thouchtless luve?
' Whase cruel heart can ettle aye
  ' Her father's dethe to pruve!'

And first he kisd her bluming cheik,
  And syne her bosom deir;
Than sadly strade athwart the ha,
  And drapd ae tendir teir.
" My meiny heid my words wi care,
  " Gin ony weit to slay
" Lord Hardyknute, by hevin I sweir
  "Wi lyfe he sall nae gae."

'My maidens bring my bridal gowne,
'I little trewd yeſtrene,
'To riſe frae bonny Draffan's bed,
'His bluidy dethe to ſene.'
Syne up to the hie baconie
She has gane wi a her train,
And ſune ſhe ſaw her ſtalwart lord
Attein the bleiſing plain.

Owr Nethan's weily ſtreim he fared
Wi ſeeming ire and pryde;
His blaſon, gliſterand owr his helm,
Bare Allan by his ſyde.
Richt ſune the bugils blew, and lang
And bludy was the fray;
Eir hour of nune, that elric tyde,
Had hundreds tint their day.

Like beacon bricht at deid of nicht,
The michty chief muvd on;
His baſnet, bleiſing to the ſun,
Wi deidly lichtning ſhone.
Draffan he ſocht, wi him at anes
To end the cruel ſtryſe;
But aye his ſpeirmen thranging round
Forfend their leider's lyſe.

The winding Clyde wi valiant bluid
  Ran reiking mony a mile;
Few ſtude the faucht, yet dethe alane
  Cold end their irie toil.
'Wha flie, I vow, ſall frae my ſpeir
  'Receive the dethe they dreid!'
Cryd Draffan, as alang the plain
  He ſpurd his bluid-red ſteid.

Up to him ſune a knicht can prance,
  A graith'd in ſilver mail:
"Lang have I ſocht thee throuch the field,
  "This lance will tell my tale."
Rude was the fray, till Draffan's ſkill
  Oercame his youthful micht;
Perc'd throuch the viſor to the eie
  Was ſlayne the comly knicht.

The viſor on the ſpeir was deft,
  And Draffan Malcolm ſpied;
'Ye ſhould your vaunted ſpeid this day,
  'And not your ſtrenth, ha ſey'd.'
"Cative, awa ye maun na flie,"
  Stout Rothſay cry'd bedeen,
"Till, frae my glaive, ye wi ye beir
  "The wound ye fein'd yeſtrene."

'Mair

'Mair o your kins bluid ha I ſpilt
'Than I docht evir grein;
'See Rothſay whar your brither lyes
'In dethe afore your eyne.'
Bold Rothſay cried wi lion's rage,
"O hatefu curſed deid!
"Sae Draffan ſeiks our ſiſter's luve,
"Nor feirs far ither meid!"

Swith on the word an arrow cam
Frae ane o Rothſay's band,
And ſmote on Draffan's liſted targe,
Syne Rothſays ſplent it fand.
Perc'd throuch the knie to his ferce ſteid,
Wha pranc'd wi egre pain,
The chief was forcd to quit the ſtryfe,
And ſeik the nether plain.

His minſtrals there wi dolefu care
The bludy ſhaft withdrew;
But that he ſae was bar'd the fecht
Sair did the leider rue.
'Cheir ye my mirrie men,' Draffan cryd,
Wi meikle pryde and glie;
'The priſe is ours; nae chieftan bides
'Wi us to bate the grie.'

That hautie boaſt heard Hardyknute,
  Whar he lein'd on his ſpeir,
Sair weiried wi the nune-tide heat,
  And toilſum deids of weir.
The firſt ſicht, when he paſt the thrang,
  Was Malcolm on the ſwaird:
" Wold hevin that dethe my eild had tane,
  " And thy youtheid had ſpard!

" Draffan I ken thy ire, but now
  " Thy micht I mein to ſee."
But eir he ſtrak the deidly dint
  The ſyre was on his knie.
' Lord Hardyknute ſtryke gif ye may,
  ' I neir will ſtryve wi thee;
' Forfend your dochter ſee you ſlayne
  ' Frae whar ſhe ſits on hie!

' Yeſtrene the prieſt in haly band
  ' Me join'd wi Fairly deir;
' For her ſake let us part in peace,
  ' And neir meet mair in weir.'
" Oh king of hevin, what ſeimly ſpeech
  " A featour's lips can ſend!
" And art thou he wha baith my ſons
  " Brocht to a bluidy end?

" Haſte

" Haſte, mount thy ſteid, or I ſall licht
 " And meit thee on the plain ;
" For by my forbere's ſaul we neir
 " Sall part till ane be ſlayne."
' Now mind thy aith,' ſyne Draffan ſtout
 To Allan loudly cryd,
Wha drew the ſhynand blade bot dreid
 And perc'd his maſters ſyde.

Law to the bleiding eard he fell,
 And dethe ſune clos'd his eyne.
" Draffan, till now I did na ken
 " Thy dethe cold muve my tein.
" I wold to Chryſte thou valiant youth,
 " Thou wert in life again ;
" May ill befa my ruthleſs wrauth
 " That brocht thee to ſic pain !

" Fairly, anes a my joy and pryde,
 " Now a my grief and bale,
" Ye maun wi haly maidens byde
 " Your deidly faut to wail.
" To Icolm beir ye Draffan's corſe,
 " And dochter anes ſae deir,
" Whar ſhe may pay his heidles luve
 " Wi mony a mournfu teir."

II. CHILD MAURICE.

I.

CHILD MAURICE was an erle's son,
His name it waxed wide;
It was nae for his great riches,
Nor yit his meikle pride,
But it was for his mother gay
Wha livd on Carron side.

II.

'Whar sall I get a bonny boy,
'That will win hose and shoen,
'That will gae to lord Barnard's ha,
'And bid his lady come?

III.

'And ye maun rin errand Willie,
'And ye maun rin wi speid;
'When ither boys gang on their feet
'Ye sall ha prancing steid.'

IV.

"Oh no! oh no! my master deir!
"I dar na for my life;
"I'll no gae to the bauld barons,
"For to triest furth his wife."

V. 'My

V.

‘ My bird Willie, my boy Willie,
‘ My deir Willie,’ he ſaid,
‘ How can ye ſtrive againſt the ſtreim ?
‘ For I ſall be obeyd.’

VI.

“ But O my maſter deir !” he cryd,
“ In grenewode ye're your lane ;
“ Gi owr ſic thochts I wald ye red,
“ For feir ye ſold be tane.”

VII.

‘ Haſte, haſte, I ſay, gae to the ha,
‘ Bid her come here wi ſpeid ;
‘ If ye refuſe my hie command,
‘ I'll gar your body bleid.

VIII.

‘ Gae bid her tak this gay mantel,
‘ Tis a gowd but the hem :
‘ Bid her come to the gude grenewode,
‘ Ein by herſel alane :

IX.

‘ And there it is, a ſilken ſarke,
‘ Her ain hand ſewd the ſleeve ;
‘ And bid her come to Child Maurice ;
‘ Speir nae bauld baron's leive.’

X.

"Yes I will gae your black errand,
"Thouch it be to your coſt;
"Sen ye will nae be warnd by me,
"In it ye ſall find froſt.

XI.

"The baron he's a man o micht,
"He neir cold bide to taunt:
"And ye will ſee before its nicht,
"Sma cauſe ye ha to vaunt.

XII.

"And ſen I maun your errand rin,
"Sae ſair againſt my will,
"I'ſe mak a vow, and keip it trow,
"It ſall be done for ill."

XIII.

Whan he cam to the broken brig,
He bent his bow and ſwam;
And whan he came to graſs growing,
Set down his feet and ran.

XIV.

And whan he cam to Barnards yeat,
Wold neither chap nor ca,
But ſet his bent bow to his breiſt,
And lichtly lap the wa.

XV.

He wald na tell the man his errand
  Thoch he ſtude at the yeat ;
But ſtreight into the ha he cam,
  Whar they were ſet at meat.

XVI.

' Hail ! hail ! my gentle ſire and dame !
  ' My meſſage winna wait,
' Dame ye maun to the grenewode gae,
  ' Afore that it be late.

XVII.

' Ye're bidden tak this gay mantel,
  ' Tis a gowd bot the hem :
' Ye maun haſte to the gude grenewode,
  ' Ein by yourſell alane.

XVIII.

' And there it is, a ſilken ſark,
  ' Your ain hand ſewd the ſleive ;
' Ye maun gae ſpeik to Child Maurice ;
  ' Speir na bauld baron's leive.'

XIX.

The lady ſtamped wi her foot,
  And winked wi her eie ;
But a that ſhe cold ſay or do,
  Forbidden he wald nae be.

XX.

" It's ſurely to my bower-woman,
" It neir cold be to me."
' I brocht it to lord Barnard's lady,
' I trow that ye be ſhe.'

XXI.

Then up and ſpak the wylie nurſe,
(The bairn upon her knie),
" If it be come from Child Maurice
" It's deir welcum to me."

XXII.

' Ye lie, ye lie, ye filthy nurſe,
' Sae loud as I heir ye lie;
' I brocht it to lord Barnard's lady
' I trow ye be nae ſhee.'

XXIII.

Then up and ſpake the bauld baron
An angry man was he:
He has tane the table wi his foot,
Sae has he wi his knie,
Till cryſtal cup and ezar diſh
In flinders he gard flie.

XXIV.

" Gae bring a robe of your cliding,
" Wi a the haſte ye can,
" And I'll gae to the gude grenewode,
" And ſpeik wi your lemman."

XXV. ' O bide

XXV.

'O bide at hame now lord Barnard!
  'I ward ye bide at hame;
'Neir wyte a man for violence,
  'Wha neir wyte ye wi nane.'

XXVI.

Child Maurice ſat in the grenewode,
  He whiſtled and he ſang:
"O what meins a the folk coming?
  "My mother tarries lang."

XXVII.

The baron to the grenewode cam,
  Wi meikle dule and care;
And there he firſt ſpyd Child Maurice,
  Kaming his yellow hair.

XXVIII.

'Nae wonder, nae wonder, Child Maurice,
  'My lady loes thee weil:
'The faireſt part of my body
  'Is blacker than thy heil.

XXIX.

'Yet neir the leſs now, Child Maurice,
  'For a thy great bewtie,
'Ye'ſe rew the day ye eir was born;
  'That head ſall gae wi me.'

XXX.

Now he has drawn his truſty brand,
  And ſlaided owr the ſtrae;
And throuch Child Maurice fair body
  He gar'd the cauld iron gae.

XXXI.

And he has tane Child Maurice heid,
  And ſet it on a ſpeir;
The meineſt man in a his train
  Has gotten that heid to beir.

XXXII.

And he has tane Child Maurice up,
  Laid him acroſs his ſteid;
And brocht him to his painted bower
  And laid him on a bed.

XXXIII.

The lady on the caſtle wa
  Beheld baith dale and down;
And there ſhe ſaw Child Maurice heid
  Cum trailing to the toun.

XXXIV.

" Better I loe that bluidy heid,
  " Bot and that yellow hair,
" Than lord Barnard and a his lands
  " As they lig here and there."

XXXV.

And ſhe has tane Child Maurice heid,
 And kiſſed baith cheik and chin;
" I was anes fow of Child Maurice.
 " As the hip is o the ſtane.

XXXVI.

" I gat ye in my father's houſe
 " Wi meikle ſin and ſhame;
" I brocht ye up in the grenewode
 " Ken'd to myſell alane:

XXXVII.

" Aft have I by thy craddle ſitten,
 " And fondly ſein thee ſleip;
" But now I maun gae 'bout thy grave
 " A mother's teirs to weip."

XXXVIII.

Again ſhe kiſs'd his bluidy cheik,
 Again his bluidy chin;
" O better I loed my ſon Maurice,
 " Than a my kyth and kin!"

XXXIX.

' Awa, awa, ye ill woman,
 ' An ill dethe may ye die!
' Gin I had ken'd he was your ſon
 ' He had neir been ſlayne by me.'

XL.

" Obraid me not, my lord Barnard!
" Obraid me not for ſhame!
" Wi that ſam ſpeir, O perce my heart,
" And ſave me frae my pain!

XLI.

" Since nothing but Child Maurice head
" Thy jealous rage cold quell,
" Let that ſame hand now tak her lyfe,
" That neir to thee did ill.

XLII.

" To me nae after days nor nichts
" Will eir be ſaft or kind:
" I'll fill the air wi heavy ſichs,
" And greit till I be blind."

XLIII.

' Eneuch of bluid by me's been ſpilt,
' Seek not your dethe frae me;
' I'd rather far it had been myſel,
' Than either him or thee.

XLIV.

' Wi hopeleſs wae I hear your plaint,
' Sair, ſair, I rue the deid.—
' That eir this curſed hand of mine
' Sold gar his body bleid!

XLV. ' Dry

XLV.

'Dry up your teirs, my winſome dame,
'They neir can heal the wound;
'Ye ſee his heid upon the ſpeir,
'His heart's bluid on the ground.

XLVI.

'I curſe the hand that did the deid,
'The heart that thocht the ill,
'The feet that bare me wi ſic ſpeid,
'The comlie youth to kill.

XLVII.

'I'll aye lament for Child Maurice
'As gin he war my ain;
'I'll neir forget the dreiry day
'On which the youth was ſlain.'

III. ADAM O GORDON.

I.

IT fell about the Martinmas,
Whan the wind blew ſhrill and cauld:
Said Adam o Gordon to his men,
" We maun draw to a hauld.

II.

" And what a hauld ſall we draw to,
" My mirrie men and me?
" We will gae ſtrait to Towie houſe
" And ſee that fair ladie."

III.

The lady on her caſtle wa
Beheld baith dale and down,
When ſhe was ware of a hoſt of men
Riding toward the toun.

IV.

'O fee ye not, my mirry men a,
'O fee ye not what I fee?
'Methinks I fee a hoft of men,
'I marvel wha they be.'

V.

She wein' it had been her luvely lord,
As he came ryding hame;
It was the traitor Adam o Gordon,
Wha reck'd nae fin or fhame.

VI.

She had nae funer bufked herfel,
And putten on her gown,
Than Adam o Gordon and his men
Were round about the toun.

VII.

The lady ran to hir touir heid
Sae faft as fhe cold drie,
To fee if by her fpeiches fair
She cold wi him agree.

VIII.

But whan he faw the lady fafe,
And the yates a locked faft,
He fell into a rage of wrauth,
And his heart was all aghaft.

IX. "Cum

IX.

" Cum doun to me ye lady gay,
  " Cum doun, Cum doun to me:
" This nicht ye sall lye in my arms,
  " The morrow my bride sall be."

X.

' I winna cum doun ye fause Gordon,
  ' I winna cum doun to thee;
' I winna forsake my ain deir lord,
  ' Thouch he is far frae me.'

XI.

" Give owr your house, ye lady fair,
  " Give owr your house to me;
" Or I sall brin yoursel therein,
  " Bot and your babies thrie."

XII.

' I winna give owr, ye fause Gordon,
  ' To nae sic traitor as thee;
' And if ye brin me and my babes,
  ' My lord sall mak ye drie.

XIII.

' But reach my pistol, Glaud my man,
  ' And charge ye weil my gun,
' For, bot if I perce that bluidy butcher,
  ' We a sall be undone.'

XIV.

She ſtude upon the caſtle wa
  And let twa bullets flie;
She miſt that bluidy butchers heart,
  And only razd his knie.

XV.

" Set fire to the houſe," cryd fauſe Gordon,
  A wood wi dule and ire;
" Fauſe lady ye ſall rue this deid
  " As ye brin in the fire."

XVI.

' Wae worth, wae worth ye Jock my man,
  ' I paid ye weil your fee;
' Why pow ye out the ground-wa ſtane
  ' Lets in the reik to me?

XVII.

' And ein wae worth ye Jock my man
  ' I paid ye weil your hire;
' Why pow ye out the ground wa ſtane
  ' To me lets in the fire?'

XVIII.

" Ye paid me weil my hire, lady,
  " Ye paid me weil my fee:
" But now I'm Adam o Gordon's man;
  " And maun or doe or die."

XIX. O

XIX.

O than befpak her little fon
  Frae aff the nource's knie,
' Oh mither deir, gi owr this houfe,
  ' For the reik it fmithers me!'

XX.

" I wald gie a my gowd, my chyld,
  " Sae wald I a my fee,
" For ae blaft o the weftlin wind,
  " To blaw the reik frae thee."

XXI.

O than befpak her dochter deir,
  She was baith jimp and fma,
' O row me in a pair o fheits,
  ' And tow me owr the wa.'

XXII.

They rowd her in a pair o fheits,
  And towd her our the wa,
But on the point o Gordon's fpeir,
  She gat a deidly fa.

XXIII.

O bonnie bonnie was her mouth,
  And chirry were her cheiks;
And cleir cleir was her yellow hair,
  Wharon the red bluid dreips!

XXIV.

Than wi his ſpeir he turnd her owr—
O gin her face was wan!
Quoth he, " Ye are the firſt that eir
" I wiſhd alive again."

XXV.

He turnd her our and our again—
O gin her ſkin was white!
" I micht ha ſpair'd that bonny face
" To hae been ſum mans delyte.

XXVI.

" Buſk and bown, my mirry men a,
" For ill doom I do gueſs:
" I canna luik on that bonnie face,
" As it lyes on the graſs."

XXVII.

'Wha luik to freits, my maſter deir,
'Freits will ay follow them:
'Let it neir be ſaid, Adam o Gordon
'Was daunted by a dame.'

XXVIII.

But whan the lady ſaw the fire
Cum flaming our her heid,
She weip'd, and kiſt her children twain;
" My bairns we been but deid."

XXIX.

The Gordon than his bugil blew,
And ſaid, ‘ Awa, awa :
‘ Sen Towie Houſe is a in a flame,
‘ I hauld it time to ga.’

XXX.

O than beſpied her ain deir lord,
As he cam owr the lee ;
He ſaw his caſtle in a blaze
Sae far as he cold ſee.

XXXI.

Then ſair, O ſair, his mind miſgave,
And a his heart was wae ;
“ Put on, put on, my wichty men,
“ Sae faſt as ye can gae.

XXXII.

“ Put on, put on, my wichty men,
“ Sae faſt as ye can drie.
“ He that is hindmoſt o the thrang
“ Sall neir get gude o me.”

XXXIII.

Than ſum they rode, and ſum they ran,
Fu faſt outowr the bent,
But eir the formoſt could win up
Baith lady and babes were brent.

XXXIV.

XXXIV.

He wrang his hands, he rent his hair,
And weipt in teinfu mude:
" Ah traitors, for this cruel deid
" Ye fall weip teirs o bluid!"

XXXV.

And after the Gordon he has gane,
Sae faſt as he micht drie:
And ſune in his foul hartis bluid
He has wreken his deir ladie.

IV. The CHILD of ELLE.

I.

ON yonder hill a caſtle ſtandes,
With walles and towres bedight;
And yonder lives the Child of Elle,
A younge and comely knighte.

II.

The Child of Elle to his garden wente,
And ſtood at his garden pale,
Whan, lo, he beheld fair Emmeline's page
Come tripping doune the dale.

III.

The Child of Elle he hyed him thence,
Y-wis he ſtoode not ſtille,
And ſoone he mette faire Emmeline's page
Come climbing up the hille.

IV.

Now Chriſte thee ſave thou little foot page,
Now Chriſte thee ſave and ſee,
Oh telle me how does thy ladye gaye,
And what may thy tydinges be?

V. My

V.

My lady ſhe is all woe-begone,
And the teares they fall from her eyne;
And aye ſhe laments the deadly feude
Betweene her houſe and thine.

VI.

And here ſhee ſends thee a ſilken ſcarfe,
Bedewde with many a teare;
And biddes thee ſometimes think on her
Who loved thee ſo deare.

VII.

And here ſhee ſends thee a ring of gold,
The laſt boon thou mayſt have;
And biddes thee weare it for her ſake
Whan ſhe is laid in grave.

VIII.

For ah! her gentle heart is broke,
And in grave ſoone muſt ſhee bee,
Sith her father hath choſe her a new love,
And forbidde her to think of thee.

IX.

Her father hath brought her a carliſh knight,
Sir John of the north countraye,
And within three dayes ſhe muſt him wedde,
Or he vowes he will her ſlaye.

X.

Now hye thee backe, thou little foot page,
And greet thy ladye from mee.
And telle her that I, her owne true love,
Will dye or ſette her free.

XI.

Now hye thee backe, thou little foot page,
And let thy fair ladye know
This night will I be at her bowre-windowe,
Betide me weale or woe.

XII.

The boye he tripped, the boye he ranne,
He neither ſtint na ſtayd,
Untill he came to fair Emmeline's bowre,
Whan kneeling downe he ſayd;

XIII.

O, ladye, I've been with thy own true love,
And he greets thee well by mee;
This night will he bee at thy bowre windowe,
And die or ſett thee free.

XIV.

Now day was gone and night was come,
And all were faſt aſleepe:
All ſave the lady Emmeline,
Who ſate in her bowre to weepe.

XV.

And ſune ſhe heard her true love's voice,
 Lowe whiſpering at the walle;
Awake, awake, my dear ladye,
 'Tis I thy true love call.

XVI.

Awake, awake my ladye deare,
 Come mount this fair palfraye;
This ladder of ropes will lette thee downe,
 Ile carrye thee hence awaye.

XVII.

Now naye, now naye, thou gentle knight,
 Now naye this may not bee;
For aye ſhould I tine my maiden fame,
 If alone I ſhould wend with thee.

XVIII.

O ladye thou with a knight ſo true
 Mayſt ſafelye wend alone,
To my lady mother I will thee bring,
 Where marriage ſhall make us one.

XIX.

" My father he is a baron bolde,
 " Of lynage proud and hye,
" And what would he ſaye if his daughter
 " Awaye with a knight ſhould fly?

XX.

" Ah well I wot he never would reſt,
  " Nor his meate ſhould do him no goode,
" Till he had ſlayne thee, Child of Elle,
  " And ſeene thy deare heart's bloode."

XXI.

O, lady, wert thou in thy ſaddle ſet,
  And a little ſpace him fro,
I would not care for thy cruel father,
  Nor the worſt that he could doe.

XXII.

O, lady, wert thou in thy ſaddle ſette,
  And once without this walle,
I would not care for thy cruel father,
  Nor the worſt that might befalle.

XXIII.

Fair Emmeline ſigh'd, fair Emmeline wept,
  And aye her heart was woe,
At lengthe he ſeizde her lilly-white hand,
  And doune the ladder he drewe.

XXIV.

And thrice he claſpde her to his breſte,
  And kiſt her tenderlie;
The tears that fell from her fair eyes
  Ranne like the fountayne free.

XXV.

He mounted himſelfe on his ſteede ſo talle,
And her on a fair palfraye,
And flung his bugle about his necke,
And roundlye they rode awaye.

XXVI.

All this beheard her own damſelle,
In her bed whereas ſhe lay,
Quoth ſhee, My lord ſhall knowe of this
So I ſhall have golde and fee.

XXVII.

Awake, awake, thou baron bold!
Awake, my noble dame!
Your daughter is fledde with the Child of Elle,
To doe the deede of ſhame.

XXVIII.

The baron he woke, the baron he roſe,
And callde his merry men all;
"And come thou forth, Sir John the knighte,
"The ladye is carried to thrall."

XXIX.

Fair Emmeline ſcant had ridden a mile,
A mile forth of the towne,
When ſhe was aware of her father's men
Come galloping over the downe.

XXX. And

XXX.

And foremoſt came the carliſh knight,
Sir John of the north countraye,
" Nowe ſtop, nowe ſtop, thou falſe traitour,
" Nor carry that lady awaye.

XXXI.

" For ſhe is come of hye lynage,
" And was of a lady borne;
" And ill it beſeems thee a falſe churles's ſonne,
" To carry her hence to ſcorne."

XXXII.

Now loud thou lyeſt, Sir John the knight,
Nowe thou doeſt lye of mee;
A knight me gott, and a ladye me bore,
Soe never did none by thee.

XXXIII.

But light nowe doune, my lady faire,
Light down and hold my ſteed,
While I and this diſcourteous knighte
Do try this arduous deede.

XXXIV.

Fair Emmeline ſighd, fair Emmeline weept,
And aye her heart was woe;
While twixt her love and the carliſh knight,
Paſt many a baleful blow.

XXXV.

The Child of Elle he fought ſoe well,
As his weapon he wavde amaine,
That ſoone he had ſlaine the carliſh knight,
And layd him upon the playne.

XXXVI.

And now the baron and all his men
Full faſt approached nye,
Ah what maye ladye Emmeline doe?
'Twere now no boote to flye.

XXXVII.

Her lover he put his horn to his mouth,
And blew both loud and ſhrill,
And ſoone he ſawe his owne merry men
Come ryding over the hill.

XXXVIII.

Now hold thy hand thou bold baron,
I pray thee hold thy hand;
Nor ruthleſs rend two gentle hearts
Faſt knit in true love's band.

XXXIX.

Thy daughter I have dearly lovde,
Full long and many a day,
But with ſuch love as holy kirke
Hath freelye ſaid wee may.

XL.

O give consent she may be mine,
 And blesse a faithful paire;
My lands and livings are not small,
 My house and lynage faire.

XLI.

My mother she was an erle's daughter,
 And a noble knight my sire ——
The baron he frownde, and turn'd away,
 With mickle dole and ire.

XLII.

Fair Emmeline sigh'd, fair Emmeline wept,
 And did all trembling stand;
At lengthe she sprang upon her knee,
 And held his lifted hand.

XLIII.

Pardon, my lord and father deare,
 This faire yong knight and mee,
Trust me, but for the carlish knight,
 I never had fled from thee.

XLIV.

Oft have you calld your Emmaline,
 Your darling and your joye;
O let not then your harsh resolves
 Your Emmaline destroye.

XLV.

The baron he ſtroakd his dark broun cheeke,
  And turnd his heade aſyde,
To wipe awaye the ſtarting teare
  He proudly ſtrave to hyde.

XLVI.

In deep revolving thought he ſtoode,
  And mus'd a little ſpace;
Then rais'd fair Emmeline from the grounde,
  With many a fond embrace.

XLVII.

Here take her, Child of Elle, he ſayd;
  And gave her lillye hand:
Here take my deare and only child,
  And with her half my land.

XLVIII.

Thy father once mine honour wrong'd,
  In dayes of youthful pride,
Do thou the injury repayre
  In fondneſs for thy bride.

XLIX.

And as thou love her, and hold her deare,
  Heaven proſper thee and thine;
And now my bleſſing wend wi' thee
  My lovelye Emmeline.

V. GILDEROY.

V. GILDEROY.

I.

GILDEROY was a bonny boy,
Had roſes till his ſhoon;
His ſtockings were of ſilken ſoy,
Wi garters hanging doun.
It was, I ween, a comelie ſight
To ſee ſae trim a boy:
He was my joy, and heart's delight,
My handſome Gilderoy.

II.

O ſic twa charming een he had!
Breath ſweet as ony roſe:
He never ware a highland plaid,
But coſtly ſilken clothes.
He gain'd the luve of ladies gay,
Nane eer to him was coy:
Ah wae is me, I mourn the day
For my dear Gilderoy.

III. My

III.

My Gilderoy and I were born
Baith in ae toun together;
We ſcant were ſeven years beforn
We gan to luve ilk ither:
Our dadies and our mamies thay
Were fill'd wi mikle joy,
To think upon the bridal day
Of me and Gilderoy.

IV.

For Gilderoy, that luve of mine
Gude faith, I freely bought
A wedding ſark of Holland fine,
Wi dainty ruffles wrought;
And he gied me a wedding ring
Which I receiv'd wi joy:
Nae lad nor laſſie eer could ſing
Like me and Gilderoy.

V.

Wi mickle joy we ſpent our prime
Till we were baith ſixteen,
And aft we paſt the langſame time
Amang the leaves ſae green:
Aft on the banks we'd ſit us thair,
And ſweetly kiſs and toy;
While he wi garlands deck'd my hair,
My handſome Gilderoy.

VI.

Oh that he ſtill had been content
Wi me to lead his life!
But, ah, his manfu heart was bent
To ſtir in feats of ſtrife.
And he in mary a venturous deed
His courage bauld wad try;
And now this gars my heart to bleed
For my dear Gilderoy.

VII.

And when of me his leave he tuik,
The tears they wat mine ee:
I gied him ſic a parting luik!
'My beniſon gang wi thee!
'God ſpeed thee weil mine ain dear heart,
'For gane is all my joy;
'My heart is rent, ſith we maun part,
'My handſome Gilderoy.'

VIII.

My Gilderoy, baith far and near
Was fear'd in every toun;
And bauldly bare awa the geir,
Of mony a lawland loun.
For man to man durſt meet him nane,
He was ſae brave a boy;
At length wi numbers he was tane,
My winſome Gilderoy.

IX.

Wae worth the louns that made the laws
  To hang a man for gear;
To reave of life for ſic a cauſe
  As ſtealing horſe or mare!
Had not their laws been made ſae ſtrick
  I neer had loſt my joy;
Wi ſorrow neer had wat my cheek
  For my dear Gilderoy.

X.

Gif Gilderoy had done amiſs,
  He mought hae baniſht been;——
Ah what fair cruelty is this,
  To hang ſic handſome men!
To hang the flower o Scotiſh land,
  Sae ſweet and fair a boy:——
Nae lady had ſae white a hand
  As thee, my Gilderoy.

XI.

Of Gilderoy ſae fear'd they were,
  Wi irons his limbs they ſtrung;
To Edinborow led him thair,
  And on a gallows hung.
They hung him high aboon the reſt,
  He was ſae bauld a boy;
Thair dyed the youth wham I lued beſt,
  My handſome Gilderoy.

XII.

Sune as he yielded up his breath
  I bare his corſe away,
Wi tears, that trickled for his death,
  I waſh'd his comelie clay;
And ſiker in a grave right deep
  I laid the dear lued boy:
And now for ever I maun weep,
  My winſome Gilderoy.

VI.

VI.

I.

THE gypsies came to our good lord's gate;
  And vow but they sang sweetly!
Our lady came doun the music to hear,
  They sang sae very completely.

II.

And she came tripping down the stair,
  And a her maids before her;
As soon as they saw her weil-fared face,
  They coost the glamer our her.

III.

Gae tak frae me this gay mantile,
  And bring to me a plaidie;
For, if kith and kin and a had sworn,
  I'll follow the gypsie laddie.

IV.

Yestreen I lay in a weel-made bed,
  And my good lord beside me;
This night I'll ly in a tenant's barn,
  Whatever shall betide me.

V.

Oh come to your bed, ſays Johnie Fa,
  Oh come to your bed my dearie;
For I vow and ſwear by the hilt of my ſword,
  Your lord ſhall nae mair come near ye.

VI.

I'll go to bed to my Johnie Fa,
  I'll go to bed to my dearie;
For I vow and ſwear by what paſt yeſtreen,
  My lord ſhall nae mair come near me.

VII.

And when our lord came hame at een
  And ſpeird for his fair lady,
The tane ſhe cry'd, and the ither reply'd,
  She's awa wi the gypſie laddie.

VIII.

Gae ſaddle to me the black black ſteed,
  Gae ſaddle and mak him ready;
Before that I either eat or ſleep
  I'll gae and ſeek my fair lady.

IX.

And we were fifteen well-made men,
  Of courage ſtout and ſteady;
And we were a put doun, but ane,
  For a fair young wanton lady.

VII. THE

VII. THE CRUEL KNIGHT.

I.

THE knight ſtands in the ſtable door
As he was bownd to ride;
Whan out thair comes his fair lady,
And him deſires to bide.

II.

"How can I bide, how dare I bide,
"How can I bide wi thee?
"Have I not kill'd thy ae brother?
"Thou hadſt nae mair but he."

III.

'If thou haſt kill'd my ae brother,
'Alas and wae is me!
'But if I ſave thee from the paine,
'My luve's the mair to thee.'

IV.

She has taen him to her ſecret bower,
Steik'd wi a ſiller-pin;
And ſhe's up to the higheſt tower,
To watch that nane come in.

V.

She had nae weil gane up the ſtair,
And entered in the tower,
When four and twenty armed knights
Came riding to the door.

VI.

‘ Now God you ſave, my fair lady,
‘ Declare to me I pray,
‘ Did you not ſee a wounded knight
‘ Come riding by this way?

VII.

“ Yes bloody bloody was his ſword,
“ And bloody were his hands;
“ But, if the ſteed he rides be good,
“ He's paſt fair Scotland's ſtrands.”

VIII.

Then ſhe's gane to her darkſome bower,
Her huſband dear to meet;
He deem'd he heard his angry faes,
And wounded her fou deep.

IX.

‘ What harm my lord provokes thine ire,
‘ To wreak itſelf on me?
‘ Have I not ſav'd thy life frae faes,
‘ And ſav'd for ſic a fee!’

X.

“ Now live, now live, my fair lady,
 “ O live but half an hour ;
“ There's neer a leech in all Scotland
 “ But ſhall be at thy bower.”

XI.

‘ How can I live, how ſhall I live,
 ‘ How can I live for thee ?
‘ While running faſt oer a the floor,
 ‘ My heart's blood thou may'ſt ſee !’

VIII. YOUNG WATERS.

I.

ABOUT yule, quhen the wind blew eule,
  And the round tables began,
There came to wait on our king's court,
  Mony a weil-favour'd man.

II.

The Quein luik'd owr the caſtle-wa,
  Beheld baith dale and doun,
And then ſhe ſaw young Waters
  Cum riding to the town.

III.

His footmen they did rin before,
  His horſemen rade behind:
Ane mantel of the burning gowd
  Did keip him frae the wind.

IV.

Gowden-graith'd his horſe before,
  And ſiller-ſhod behind;
The horſe young Waters rode upon
  Was fleeter than the wind.

V. Up

V.

Up then ſpak a wylie lord,
And to the Queen ſaid he,
Tell me quha is the faireſt face
Rides in the companie?

VI.

I've ſeen lords, and I've ſeen lairds,
And knichts of high degree,
But a fairer face than young Waters
Mine een did never ſee.

VII.

Out then ſpak the jealous king,
(An angry man was he,)
" And if he had been twice as fair,
" You might have excepted me."

VIII.

You're neither lord, nor laird, ſhe ſays,
Bot the king that wears the crown;
There's not a knicht in fair Scotland,
Bot to thee maun bow down.

IX.

For a that ſhe could ſay or do,
Appeas'd he wad nae be;
Bot for the words that ſhe had ſaid,
Young Waters he maun die.

X.

Sune they hae taen young Waters,
  Put ſetters on his feet;
Sune they hae taen young Waters,
  And thrown in dungeon deep.

XI.

They hae taen to the heiding-hill,
  That knicht ſae fair to ſee;
And for the words the queen had ſpak
  Young Waters he did die.

IX. SIR HUGH;

OR, THE JEW's DAUGHTER.

I.

THE bonnie boys o merry Lincoln
War playin at the ba;
And wi them ſtude the ſweet Sir Hugh,
The flower amang them a.

II.

He kepped the ba there wi his foot,
And catchd it wi his knie,
Till in at the cruel Jew's window
Wi ſpeid he gard it flie.

III.

'Caſt out the ba to me, fair maid,
'Caſt out the ba to me:'—
"Ye neir ſall hae't my bonnie Sir Hugh,
"Till ye come up to me.

IV.

"Cum up ſweet Hugh, cum up dear Hugh
"Cum up and get the ba;"
'I winna cum up, I winna cum up
'Without my playferes a.'

V.

And ſhe has gane to her father's garden
Sae faſt as ſhe cold rin;
And powd an apple red and white
To wyle the young thing in.

VI.

She wyld him ſune throuch ae chamber,
And wyld him ſune throuch twa;
And neiſt they cam to her ain chamber,
The faireſt o them a.

VII.

She has laid him on a dreſſin board,
Whar ſhe was usd to dine;
And ſtack a penknife to his heart,
And dreſs'd him like a ſwine.

VIII.

She row'd him in a cake o lead,
And bade him lye and ſleip;
Syne threw him in the Jew's draw-well,
Fu fifty fathom deip.

IX.

Whan bells were rung, and maſs was ſung,
And ilka lady gaed hame;
Than ilka lady had her young ſon,
But lady Helen had nane.

X.

She row'd her mantel her about,
And ſair ſair can ſhe weip;
She ran wi ſpeid to the Jew's caſtel,
When a war faſt aſleip.

XI.

'My bonnie Sir Hugh, your mither calls,
'I pray thee to her ſpeik:'
"O lady rin to the deip draw-well
"Gin ye your ſon wad ſeik."

XII.

Lady Helen ran to the deip draw-well,
And kneel'd upon her knie;
'My bonnie Sir Hugh gin ye be here,
'I pray ye ſpeik to me;'

XIII.

"The lead is wondrous heavy mither,
"The well is wondrous deip;
"A kene penknife ſticks in my heart,
"A word I dounae ſpeik.

XIV.

"Gae hame, gae hame, my mither deir,
"Fetch me my winding ſheet;
"For again in merry Lincoln toun
"We twa ſall never meit."

X. FLODDEN FIELD;

OR, THE FLOWERS OF THE FOREST.

I.

I Have heard o lilting at the ewes milking,
Laſſes a lilting eir the break o day;
But now I hear moaning on ilka green loaning,
Sen our bra foreſters are a wed away.

II.

At bouchts in the morning nae blyth lads are ſcorning,
The laſſes are lonely, dowie, and wae;
Nae daffin, nae gabbing, but ſiching and ſabbing;
Ilk ane lifts her leglen and hies her away.

III.

At een in the gloming nae ſwankies are roaming,
'Mang ſtacks wi the laſſes at bogle to play;
For ilk ane ſits dreary, lamenting her deary;
The Flowers o the Foreſt, wha're a wed away.

IV.

In harſt at the ſheiring na yonkers are jeiring;
The banſters are lyart, runkled, and gray;
At fairs nor at preaching, nae wooing nae fleeching,
Sen our bra foreſters are a wed away.

V.

O dule for the order ſent our lads to the border!
The Engliſh for anes by gyle wan the day.
The Flowers o the Foreſt, wha ay ſhone the foremoſt,
The prime o the land lye cauld in the clay!

XI. EDWARD.

I.

WHY does your brand ſae drap wi bluid,
Edward, Edward?
Why does your brand ſae drap with bluid,
And why ſae ſad gang ye O!
O I hae killd my hauk ſae gude,
Mither, mither:
O I hae killd my hauk ſae gude;
And I had nae mair but he, O!

II.

Your haukis bluid was nevir ſae reid,
Edward, Edward.
Your haukis bluid was nevir ſae reid,
My deir ſon I tell thee O!
I hae killd my reid roan ſteid,
Mither, mither:
O I hae killd my reid roan ſteid
That erſt was fair and frie O!

III.

Your ſteid was auld, and ye hae mair,
Edward, Edward:
Your ſteid was auld, and ye hae mair,
Sum ither dule ye drie, O!
O I hae killd my fadir deir,
Mither, mither:
O I hae killd my fadir deir,
Alas! and wae is me O!

IV. What

IV.

What penance will ye drie for that,
Edward, Edward?
What penance will ye drie for that,
My deir ſon, now tell me O!
I'll ſet my feet in yonder boat;
Mither, mither:
I'll ſet my feet in yonder boat;
And I'le fare owr the ſea, O!

V.

What will ye do wi touirs and ha,
Edward, Edward?
What will ye do wi touirs and ha,
That were ſae fair to ſee, O!
I'le let them ſtand till they doun fa,
Mither, mither:
I'le let them ſtand till they doun fa,
For heir I maunae be O!

VI.

What will ye leive to bairns and wife,
Edward, Edward?
What will ye leive to bairns and wife,
When ye gang owr the ſea O!
The warld's room to beg throuch life,
Mither, mither:
The warld's room to beg throuch life,
For them I neir maun ſee, O!

VII.

What will ye leive to your mither deir,
Edward, Edward?
What will ye leive to your mither deir,
My deir ſon, now tell me O!
The curſe of hell frae me ſall ye beir,
Mither, mither:
The curſe of hell frae me ſall ye beir,
Sic counſeils ye gied me, O!

XII. SIR PATRICK SPENCE.

I.

THE King ſits in Dunfermlin toun,
Drinking the bluid-red wine:
“ Whar ſall I get a gude ſailor,
“ To ſail this ſhip o mine?”

II.

Than up and ſpak an eldern knicht,
Wha ſat at his richt knie;
‘ Sir Patrick Spence is the beſt ſailor,
‘ That ſails upon the ſea,’

III.

The king has written a braid letter,
And ſignd it wi his hand;
And ſent it to Sir Patrick Spence,
Wha walked on the ſand.

IV.

The firſt line that Sir Patrick red,
A leud lauch lauched he;
The neiſt line that Sir Patrick red
The teir blinded his eie.

V.

" O wha can he be that has don
  " This deid o ill to me,
" To ſend me at this time o yeir
  " To ſail upo the ſea?

VI.

" Mak haſte, mak haſte, my mirry men a
  " Our gude ſhip ſails the morne."
' O ſay na ſae, my maſter deir,
  ' For I feir deidly ſtorm.

VII.

' I ſaw the new moon late yeſtrene,
  ' Wi the auld moon in her arm;
' And I fear, I fear, my maſter deir,
  ' That we will cum to harm.'

VIII.

Our Scottiſh nobles were richt laith
  To weit their ſhyning ſhoen;
But lang or a the play was owr,
  They wat their heids aboon.

IX.

O lang lang may their ladies ſit
  And luik outowr the ſand,
Or eir they ſee the bonnie ſhip
  Cum ſailing to the land!

X.

Mair than haf owr to Aberdour—
 It's fifty fathom deip—
Lyes gude Sir Patrick Spence for aye
 Wi the Scots lords at his feit.

XIII. LADY BOTHWELL's LAMENT.

I.

BALOW, my babe, lye ſtill and ſleip,
It grieves me ſair to ſee thee weip;
If thou'lt be ſilent I'll be glad,
Thy maining maks my heart full ſad;
Balow my boy, thy mither's joy;
Thy father breids me great annoy.

II.

Whan he began to ſeik my luve,
And wi his ſucred words to muve;
His feining fauſe, and flattering cheir,
To me that time did nocht appeir;
But now I ſee that cruel he
Cares neither for my babe nor me.

III.

Lye ſtill, my darling, ſleip a while,
And whan thou wakeſt ſweitly ſmile;
But ſmile nae as thy father did
To cozen maids: nay, God forbid,
What yet I feir, that thou ſold leir
Thy father's heart and face to beir!

IV.

Be ſtill, my ſad one; ſpare thoſe teirs,
To weip whan thou haſt wit and yeirs;
Thy griefs are gathering to a ſum,
God grant thee patience when they cum;
Born to proclaim a mother's ſhame,
A father's fall, a baſtard's name.

XIV. THE EARL OF MURRAY.

I.

YE Hielands and ye Lawlands
O whar hae ye been?
They have slain the Earl of Murray
And laid him on the green!

II.

'Now wae be to you Huntly!
'O wharfore did ye sae?
'I bad you bring him wi you;
'But forbad you him to slay.'

III.

He was a bra galant,
And he rid at the ring;
The bonnie Earl of Murray
He micht ha been a king.

IV.

He was a bra galant,
And he playd at the ba;
The bonnie Earl of Murray
Was the flower amang them a.

V.

He was a bra galant,
  And he playd at the gluve;
The bonnie Earl of Murray
  He was the queen's luve.

VI.

O lang will his lady
  Look owr the caſtle downe,
Ere ſhe ſee the Earl of Murray
  Cum ſounding throuch the toun!

XV. SIR JAMES THE ROSE.

I.

O Heard ye o Sir James the Rose,
The young heir o Buleighan?
For he has kill'd a gallant ſquire,
Whaſe friends are out to tak him.

II.

Now he has gane to the houſe o Mar,
Whar nane might ſeik to find him;
To ſee his dear he did repair,
Weining ſhe wold befreind him.

III.

'Whar are ye gaing, Sir James,' ſhe ſaid,
'O whar awa are ye riding?'
"I maun be bound to a foreign land,
"And now I'm under hiding."

IV.

"Whar ſall I gae, whar ſall I rin,
"Whar ſall I rin to lay me?
"For I ha kill'd a gallant ſquire,
"And his friends ſeik to ſlay me."

V. 'O

V.

' O gae ye doun to yon laigh houſe,
' I ſall pay there your lawing;
' And as I am your leman trew,
" I'll meet ye at the dawing.

VI.

He turnd him richt and round about
And rowd him in his brechan:
And laid him doun to tak a ſleip,
In the lawlands o Buleighan.

VII.

He was nae weil gane out o ſicht,
Nor was he paſt Milſtrethen,
Whan four and twenty belted knichts
Cam riding owr the Leathen.

VIII.

' O ha ye ſeen Sir James the Roſe,
' The young heir o Buleighan?
' For he has kill'd a gallant ſquire,
' And we are ſent to tak him.'

IX.

" Yea, I ha ſeen Sir James,' ſhe ſaid,
" He paſt by here on Monday;
" Gin the ſteed be ſwift than he rides on,
" He's paſt the Hichts of Lundie."

X. But

X.

But as wi ſpeid they rade awa,
  She loudly cryd behind them ;
" Gin ye'll gie me a worthy meid,
  " I'll tell ye whar to find him."

XI.

' O tell fair maid, and, on our band,
  ' Ye'ſe get his purſe and brechan.'
" He's in the bank aboon the mill,
  " In the lawlands o Buleighan."

XII.

Than out and ſpak Sir John the Graham,
  Wha had the charge a keiping,
" It's neer be ſaid, my ſtalwart feres,
  " We killd him whan a ſleiping."

XIII.

They ſeized his braid ſword and his targe,
  And cloſely him ſurrounded :
" O pardon! mercy! gentlemen,"
  He then fou loudly ſounded.

XIV.

' Sic as ye gae ſic ye ſall hae
  ' Nae grace we ſhaw to thee can.'
" Donald my man, wait till I fa,
  " And ye ſall hae my brechan ;
" Ye'll get my purſe thouch fou o gowd
  " To tak me to Loch Lagan."

XV.

Syne they tuke out his bleiding heart,
And fet it on a fpeir;
Then tuke it to the houfe o Mar,
And fhawd it to his deir.

XVI.

'We cold nae gie Sir James's purfe
'We cold nae gie his brechan,
'But ye fall ha his bleeding heart
'Bot and his bleeding tartan.'

XVII.

"Sir James the Rofe, O for thy fake
"My heart is now a breaking,
"Curs'd be the day, I wrocht thy wae,
"Thou brave heir of Buleighan!"

XVIII.

Then up fhe raife, and furth fhe gaes;
And, in that hour o tein,
She wanderd to the dowie glen,
And nevir mair was fein.

XVI. The LAIRD of WOODHOUSELIE.

From Tradition.

I.

SHYNING was the painted ha
Wi gladsum torches bricht;
Full twenty gowden dames sat there,
And ilkane by a knicht:
Wi music cheir,
To please the eir,
Whan bewtie pleasd the sicht.

II.

Wi cunning skill his gentle meid
To chant, or warlike fame,
Ilk damsel to the minstrels gied
Some favorit chieftan's name:
" Sing Salton's praise,"
The lady says—
In suith she was to blame.

III.

'By my renown ye wrang me sair,'
Quoth hautie Woodhouselie,
'To praise that youth o sma report,
'And never deim on me:
'Whan ilka dame
'Her fere cold name,
'In a this companie.'

IV. The

IV.

The morn ſhe to her nourice yeed;
"O meikle do I feir,
"My lord will ſlay me, ſin yeſtrene
"I prais'd my Salton deir!
"I'll hae nae eaſe,
"Till Hevin it pleaſe,
"That I lye on my beir."

V.

'Mair wold I lay him on his beir,'
The craftie nourice ſaid;
'My ſaw gin ye will heid but anes
'That ſall nae be delaid.'
"O nourice ſay,
"And, by my fay,
"Ye ſall be weil appaid."

VI.

'Take ye this drap o deidly drug
'And put it in his cup,
'When ye gang ot the gladſum ha,
'And ſit ye doun to ſup:
'Whan he has gied
'To bed bot dreid,
'He'll never mair riſe up.'

VII. And

VII.

And ſhe has tane the deidly drug
And pat it in his cup,
Whan they gaed to the gladſum ha,
And ſat them doun to ſup:
And wi ill ſpeid
To bed he gied,
And never mair raiſe up.

VIII.

The word came to his father auld
Neiſt day by hour of dyne,
That Woodhouſelie had died yeſtrene,
And his dame had held the wyne.
Quoth he "I vow
"By Mary now,
"She ſall meit ſure propine."

IX.

Syne he has flown to our gude king.
And at his feet him layne;
'O Juſtice! Juſtice! royal liege,
'My worthy ſon is ſlayne.
'His lady's feid
'Has wrocht the deid,
'Let her receive the paine.'

X.

Sair muvit was our worthy king,
 And an angry man was he;
'Gar bind her to the deidly stake,
 'And birn her on the lie:
 'That after her
 'Na bluidy fere
 'Her reckless lord may flee.'

XI.

"O wae be to ye, nourice,
 "An ill dethe may ye drie!
"For ye prepar'd the deidly drug
 "That gard my deiry die:
 "May a the paine
 "That I darraine
 "In ill tune, licht on thee!

XII

"O bring to me my goun o black,
 "My mantel, and my pall;
"And gie five merks to the friars gray
 "To pray for my poor saul:
 "And ilka dame,
 "O gentle name,
 "Bewar o my fair fall."

XVII. LORD LIVINGSTON.

From Tradition.

I.

'GRAITH my swiftest steid,' said Livingston,
'But nane of ye gae wi me;
'For I maun awa by mysel alane
'To the foot of the grenewode tree.

II.

Up spak his dame wi meikle speid.
"My lord I red ye bide;
"I dreimd a dreiry dreim last nicht:
"Nae gude sall you betide."

III.

'What freit is this, my lady deir,
'That wald my will gainstand?'
"I dreimd that I gaed to my bouir dore,
"And a deid man tuke my hand."

IV.

'Suith dreims are scant,' said the proud baron,
And leuch wi jearing glie;
'But for this sweit kiss my winsum dame
'Neist time dreim better o me.'

V. 'For

V.

' For I hecht to meit with lord Rothmar,
' To chase the fallow deer;
' And speid we weil, by the our o nune,
' We sall return bot feir.'

VI.

Frae his fair lady's sicht he strave
His ettling sae to hide;
But frae the grenewode he came nae back,
Sin eir that deidly tide.

VII.

For Rothmar met him there bot fail,
And bluidy was the strife;
Lang eir the nunetide mess was rung,
They baith war twin'd o life.

VIII.

' Forgie, forgie me, Livingston!
' That I lichtly set by your dame;
' For surely in a the warld lives not
' A lady mair free frae blame.

IX.

' Accursed be my lawles luve
' That wrocht us baith sic tein!'
" As I forgie my freind anes deir,
" Sae may I be forgien.

X.

"Thouch ye my counseil sold ha tane
 "The gait of gyle to eschew;
"Yet may my saul receive sic grace
 "As I now gie to you."

XI.

The lady in her mournfu bouir
 Sat wi richt heavy cheir,
In ilka sough that the laigh wind gied
 She weind her deir lord to heir.

XII.

Whan the sun gaed down, and mirk nicht came,
 O teirfu were her eyne!
'I feir, I feir, it was na for nocht
 'My dreims were sae dowie yestrene!'

XIII.

Lang was the nicht, but whan the morn cam,
 She said to her menie ilk ane;
'Haste, saddle your steids, and seik the gerenewode,
 'For I feir my deir lord is slain.'

XIV

Richt sune they fand their lord and Rothmar
 Deid in ilk ither's arm:
'I guess my deir lord that luve of my name
 'Alane brocht thee to sic harm.

XV.

‘ Neir will I forget thy feimly meid,
 ‘ Nor yet thy gentle luve ;
‘ For fevin lang yeirs my weids of black
 ‘ That I luvd thee as weil fall pruve.’

XVIII. BINNORIE.

From Tradition.

To preserve the tone as well as the sense of this Ballad, the burden should be repeated through the whole, though it is here omitted for the sake of conciseness.

THERE were twa sisters liv'd in a bouir;
Binnorie, O Binnorie!
Their father was a baron of pouir,
By the bonnie mildams of Binnorie.
The youngest was meek, and fair as the May,
Whan she springs in the east wi the gowden day:
The eldest austern as the winter cauld,
Ferce was her saul, and her seiming was bauld.
A gallant squire cam sweet Isabel to wooe;
Her sister had naething to luve I trow;
But filld was she wi dolour and ire,
To see that to her the comlie squire
Preferd the debonair Isabel:
Their hevin of luve of spyte was her hell.
Till ae ein she to her sister can say
"Sweit sister cum let us wauk and play."
They wauked up, and they wauked down,
Sweit sang the birdis in the vallie loun!

Whan they cam to the roaring lin,
She drave unweiting Iſabel in,
'O ſiſter! ſiſter! tak my hand,
'And ye ſall hae my ſilver fan;
'O ſiſter! ſiſter! tak my middle,
'And ye ſall hae my gowden girdle.'
Sumtimes ſhe ſank, ſumtimes ſhe ſwam,
Till ſhe cam to the miller's dam:
The miller's dochter was out that ein
And ſaw her rowing down the ſtreim.
"O father deir! in your mill dam
"There is either a lady or a milk white ſwan!"
Twa days were gane whan to her deir
Her wraith at deid of nicht cold apeir:
'My luve, my deir, how can ye ſleip,
'Whan your Iſabel lyes in the deep?
'My deir, how can ye ſleip bot pain,
'Whan ſhe by her cruel ſiſter is ſlain?'
Up raiſe he ſune in frichtfu mude,
'Buſk ye my meiny and ſeik the ſlude.'
They ſocht her up and they ſocht her doun,
And ſpyd at laſt her gliſterin gown:
They rais'd her wi richt meikle care;
Pale was her cheik, and grein was her hair!
'Gae, ſaddle to me my ſwifteſt ſteid,
'Her fere, by my fae, for her dethe ſall bleid.'
A page cam rinning out owr the lie,
"O heavie tiding I bring!" quoth he,

"My luvely lady is far awa gane,
"We weit the fairy hae her tane;
"Her ſiſter gaed wood wi' dule and rage,
"Nocht cold we do her mind to ſuage.
"O Iſabel! my ſiſter!" ſhe wold cry,
'For thee will I weip, for thee will I die!"
"Till late yeſtreene in an elric hour
"She lap frae aft the hicheſt touir"——
'Now ſleip ſhe in peace!' quoth the gallant Squire,
'Her dethe was the maiſt that I cold require:
'But I'll main for the my Iſabel deir,
'Binnorie, O Binnorie!
'Full mony a dreiry dyy, bot weir,
'By the bonnie mildams of Binnorie.'

XIX. THE DEATH OF MENTEITH.

From TRADITION.

I.

SHRILLY ſhriek'd the raging wind,
  And rudelie blew the blaſt;
Wi awſum blink, throuch the dark ha,
  The ſpeidy lichtning paſt.

II.

‘ O hear ye nae, frae mid the loch,
  ‘ Ariſe a deidly grane?
‘ Sae evir does the ſpirit warn,
  ‘ Whan we ſum dethe maun mane.

III.

‘ I feir, I feir me, gude Sir John,
  ‘ Ye are nae ſafe wi me:
‘ What wae wald ſill my heart gin ye
  ‘ Sold in my caſtle drie!’

IV.

“ Ye neid nae feir, my leman deir,
  “ I'm ay ſafe when wi thee;
“ And gin I maun nae wi thee live,
  “ I here wad wiſh to die.”

V.

His man cam rinning to the ha
  Wi wallow cheik belyve:
' Sir John Menteith, your faes are neir,
  ' And ye maun flie or ſtrive.

VI.

" What count ſyne leads the cruel knicht?"
  ' Thrie ſpeirmen to your ane:
' I red ye flie, my maſter deir,
  ' Wi ſpeid, or ye'll be ſlain.'

VII.

" Tak ye this gown, my deir Sir John,
  " To hide your ſhyning mail:
" A boat waits at the hinder port
  " Owr the braid loch to ſail."

VIII.

" O whatten a piteous ſhriek was yon
  " That ſough'd upo my eir?"
' Nae piteous ſhriek I trow, ladie,
  ' Bot the rouch blaſt ye heir.'

IX.

They ſocht the caſtle, till the morn,
  Whan they were bown'd to gae,
They ſaw the boat turn'd on the loch,
  Sir John's corſe on the brae.

XX. LORD AIRTH's COMPLAINT.

From a MANUSCRIPT.

I.

IF these ſad thoughts could be expreſs'd,
Wharwith my mind is now poſſeſs'd,
My paſſion micht, diſclos'd, have reſt,
My griefs reveal'd micht flie;
But ſtill that mind which dothe forbere
To yield a groan, a ſich, or teire,
May by its prudence, much I fear,
Encreaſe it's miſerie.

II.

My heart which ceaſes now to plaine,
To ſpeke it's griefs in mournful ſtraine,
And by ſad accents eaſe my paine,
Is ſtupefied with woe.
For leſſer cares doe murne and crie,
While greater cares are mute and die;
As iſſues run a fountain drie,
Which ſtop'd wold overflow.

III. My

III.

My fichs are fled; no teirs now rin,
But fwell to whelm my foul within,
How pitieful the cafe I'm in,
Admire but doe not trie.
My croffes I micht juftly pruve,
Are common forrows far abuve;
My griefs ay in a circle muve,
And will doe till I die.

XXI.

From TRADITION.

I.

I WISH I were where Helen lies!
Night and day on me ſhe cries
To bear her company.
O would that in her darkſome bed
My weary frame to reſt were laid
From love and anguiſh free!

II.

I hear, I hear the welcome ſound
Break ſlowly from the trembling mound
That ever calls on me:
Oh bleſſed virgin! could my power
Vye with my wiſh, this very hour
I'd ſleep death's ſleep with thee.

III.

A lover's ſigh, a lover's tear,
Attended on thy timeleſs bier:
What more can fate require?
I hear, I hear the welcome ſound—
Yes, I will ſeek the ſacred ground,
And on thy grave expire.

IV. The

IV.

The worm now taſtes that roſy mouth,
Where glowed, ſhort time, the ſmiles of youth;
And in my heart's dear home,
Her ſnowey boſom, loves to lye.—
I hear, I hear the welcome cry!
I come, my love! I come.

V.

O life begone! thy irkſome ſcene
Can bring no comfort to my pain:
Thy ſcenes my pain recall!
My joy is grief, my life is dead,
Since ſhe for whom I lived is fled;
My love, my hope, my all.

VI.

Take, take me to thy lovely ſide,
Of my loſt youth thou only bride!
O take me to thy tomb!
I hear, I hear the welcome ſound!
Yes life can fly at ſorrow's wound.
I come, I come, I come.

FRAGMENTS.

I.

EARL Douglas then wham nevir knicht
 Had valour mair nae courtesie,
Is now sair blam'd by a the land
 For lichtlying o his gay ladie.

* * * * *

'Gae little page, and tell my lord,
 'Gin he will cum and dyne wi me,
'I'll set him on a seat o gowd,
 'And serve him on my bended knie.'

* * * * *

'Now wae betide ye black Fastness,
 'Bot and an ill deid may ye die!
'Ye was the first and formost man
 'Wha pairted my true lord and me.'

* * * * *

II. She

II.

* * * * * * * *

She has called to her her bouir maidens,
 She has called them ane by ane:
" There lyes a deid man in my bouir,
 " I wish that he war gane."

They ha booted him and spurred him,
 As he was wont to ryde,
A hunting horn ty'd round his waist,
 A sharp sword by his syde.

Then up and spak a bonnie bird,
 That sat upo the trie;
' What hae ye done wi Earl Richard,
 ' Ye was his gay ladie?'

" Cum doun, cum doun, my bonnie bird,
 " And licht upo my hand;
" And ye shall hae a cage o gowd,
 " Whar ye hae but the wand."

' Awa, awa, ye ill woman!
 ' Nae cage o gowd for me;
' As ye hae done to Earl Richard,
 ' Sae wad ye doe to me.'

* * * * * * *

III. See

III.

See ye the caſtle's lonelie wa,
  That riſes in yon yle?
There Angus mourns that eir he did
  His ſovereign's luve begyle.

* * * * * * * *

' O will ye gae wi me fair maid?
  ' O will ye gae wi me?
' I'll ſet you in a bouir o gowd
  ' Nae haly cell ye'ſe drie.'

" O meikle lever wald I gang
  " To bide for ay wi thee,
" Then heid the king my father's will,
  " The haly cell to drie.

" Sin I maun nevir ſee nor ſpeke
  " Wi him I luve ſae deir,
" Ye are the firſt man in the land
  " I wald cheis for my fere."

* * * * * * *

IV.

Whar yon cleir burn frae down the loch,
Rins faftlie to the fea,
There latelie bath'd in hete o nune
A fquire of valour hie.

He kend nae that the faufe mermaid
There us'd to beik and play,
Or he had neir gane to the bathe,
I trow, that dreirie day.

Nae funer had he deft his claiths,
Nae funer gan to fwim,
Than up fhe rais'd her bonnie face
Aboon the glittering ftreim.

' O comelie youth, gin ye will cum
' And be my leman deir,
' Ye fall ha pleafance o ilk fort,
' Bot any end or feir.

' I'll tak ye to my emraud ha
' Wi perles lichted round;
' Whar ye fall live wi luve and me,
' And neir by bale be found.

* * * * * * * *

NOTES.

NOTES.

HARDYKNUTE.

PART I.

HARDYKNUTE.] This name is of *Daniſh* extract, and ſignifies *Canute the ſtrong*. *Hardy* in the original implies *ſtrong*, not *valiant*; and though uſed in the latter ſenſe by the Engliſh, yet the Scots ſtill take it in its firſt acceptation. "The names in "Cunningham," ſays Sir David Dalrymple, "are all "Saxon, as is the name of the country itſelf." Annals of Scotland, *an.* 1160, *note*. The *Daniſh* and *Saxon* are both derived from the old *Gothic*, and were ſo ſimilar, that a perſon of the one nation might underſtand one of the other ſpeaking in his proper tongue. From the names and whole tenor of this poem, I am inclined to think the chief ſcene is laid in Cunninghamſhire; where likewiſe the *battle of Largs*, ſuppoſed to be that ſo nobly deſcribed in the firſt part, was fought.

Ver. 5. *Britons.*] This was the common name which the Scots gave the Engliſh anciently, as may be obſerved in their old poets; and particularly *Blind Harry*, whoſe teſtimony indeed can only be relied on, as to the common language and manners of his time; his Life of Wallace being a tiſſue of the moſt abſurd fables ever mingled.

V. 9. *Hie on a hill*, &c.] This neceſſary caution in thoſe times, when ſtrength was the only protection from violence, is well painted by a contemporary French bard:

Un chaſteau ſcay ſur roche eſpouvantable,
En lieu venteux, la rive perilleuſe,
La vy tyrant ſeant à haute table,
En grand palais, en ſal plantureuſe, &c.

D' Alliac, Eveque de Cambray.

V. 12. *Knicht.*] Theſe knights were only military officers attending the earls, barons, &c. as appears from the hiſtories of the middle ages. See Selden, *Tit. Hon. P.* II. *c.* 5. The name is of Saxon origin, and of remote antiquity, as is proved by the following fragment of a poem on the Spaniſh expedition of Charles the Great, written at that period:

Sie

Sie zeslugen ros unde man
Mit ire scarfen spiezen;
Thie gote mosen an theme plöte binnen uliezen:
Ther site was under goten kneghten,
Sic kunden wole vochten.

i. e.

Occiderunt equos et viros
Acutis suis hastis;
Deos opportuit sanguine fluere:
Hic mos erat inter nobiles *milites*,
Poterant optime pugnare.

MS. de Bello Car. M. Hisp. apud Keysler diss. de Cultu Solis, Freji, & Othini; Halæ, 1728.

The oath which the ancient knights of Scotland gave at their investiture is preserved in a letter of Drummond of Hawthornden to Ben Jonson, and is as follows:

I shall fortifie and defend the true holy Catholique and Christian Religion, presently professed, at all my power.

I shall be loyal and true to my Sovereign Lord the King his Majesty; and do honour and reverence to all orders of chevalrie, and to the noble office of arms.

I shall fortifie and defend justice to the uttermost of my power, but feid or favour.

I shall never flie from the King's Majesty my Lord and Master, or his lieutenant, in time of battel or medly with dishonour.

I shall defend my native country from all aliens and strangers at all my power.

I shall maintain and defend the honest actes and quarrels of all ladies of honour, widows, orphans, and maids of good fame.

I shall do diligence, wherever I hear tell there are any traitors, murtherers, rievers, and masterful theeves and outlaws, that suppress the poor, to bring them to the law at all my power.

I shall maintain and defend the noble and gallant state of chevalrie with horses, harnesses, and other knightly apparel to my power.

I shall be diligent to enquire, and seek to have the knowledge of all points and articles, touching or concerning my duty, contained in the book of chevalry.

All and sundry the premises I oblige me to keep and fulfill. So help me God by my own hand, and by God himself.

A curious account of the rise and progress of knighthood, and its influence on society, may be found in a learned and ingenious work lately published by Dr. Stuart, intitled, *A view of Society in Europe, or Enquiries concerning the History of Law, Government, and Manners.*

V. 16. *Emergard.*] In the common copies it is Elenor, and indeed in all the recitals I have heard; but in a late edition published with other Scotish songs at Edinburgh, 1776, it is rightly read as here. *Emergard,* or *Ermengarde,* was daughter of the Viscount of Beau-

mont,

mont, and wife of William the Lyon. She died in 1233 As the name was uncommon, and of difficult pronunciation, the rehearsers seem to have altered it to *Elenor*, which has none of these defects.

The battle of Largs, supposed to be that meant in this poem, was fought on the first of August 1263, so that queen Emergard was dead thirty years before; yet this can amount to no error in chronology, as the verses evidently imply that the lady of Hardyknute *had* no equal in the kingdom for beauty save the queen in the prime of the youth and beauty of both, which might well be forty years, or more, before the period of action in the poem.

V. 25. *Fairly*.] This name seems likewise of Saxon origin. There is a small island and a rivulet in Cunningham still called *Fairly isle* and *Fairly Burn*.

V. 43. *Twenty thousand glittering speirs*, &c.] This agrees with Buchanan's account, *Acho—viginti millia militum exposuit*. lib. 7. Torfæus asserts this number of the Norwegians was left dead on the field; but upon what authority I know not, as the ancient relations of the battle of Largs support not his testimony. See *Johnstone's Translation of Haco's Expedition to Scotland in the year* 1263, *from the Plateyan and Frisian MSS.* printed at Copenhagen 1782.

V. 49. *Page*] The Pages in the periods of chivalry were of honourable account. The young warriors were firſt denominated *pages*, then *valets*, or *damoiſeaux*, from which degree they reached that of *ecuyer*, or *ſquire*, and from this that of *knight*. See *Du Cange*, voc. *Valeti*, & *Domicellus*. *St. Palaye*, Mem. ſur l'anc. Cheval. *P*. I.

V. 61. *He has tane a horn*; &c.] The *horn*, or *bugil*, was anciently uſed by the Scots inſtead of the trumpet. They were ſometimes richly ornamented, as appears from Lindſay's deſcription of that of Sir Robert Cochran. "The horn he wore was adorned with jewels "and precious ſtones, and tipped with fine gold at "both ends." *Hiſt. of Scotland*, J. III.

V. 88. Weſtmoreland's *ferce heir*.] *Heir*, in the old Scotiſh acceptation, ſeems derived from the Latin *herus*, and ſignifies not *apparent ſucceſſor*, but *preſent lord*. As in the following lines of *Blind Harry*:

> Of Southampton he hecht baith heir and lord.
>
> B. 7. c. 1.
>
> Of Gloceſter the huge lord and heir.
>
> B. 12. c. 1.

And in this of *Dunbar*,

> Befoir *Mahoun* the heir of hell.

V. 107—112.] This minute deſcription might lead us to ſuſpect, that a female hand had ſome part in this compoſition. But, before our minſtrel, Homer has ſhewn himſelf

himſelf an adept in the lady's dreſs. To the curious remarks on the variation of the Britiſh habit, given us by Mr. Walpole, in his *Anecdotes of Painting*, and Mr. Granger, in his *Biographical Hiſtory*, might be added the following notice from a reverend miniſter of the church of Scotland. "About 1698 the women got a cuſtome of "wearing few garments: I myſelfe have ſeen the young "briſk ladies walking on the ſtreets with maſks on their "faces, and with one onlie thin petticoat and their "ſmoak; ſo thin that one would make a conſcience of "ſweiring they were not naked." *Miſcellanies, by Mr. John Bell, miniſter at Gladſmuir*, MS. pen. Edit. *title* Apparel.

V. 112. *Save that of Fairly fair.*] Working at the needle, &c. was reckoned an honourable employment by the greateſt ladies of thoſe times. Margaret, the queen of Malcolm III. as we learn from her life written by *Turgot* her confeſſor, employed the leiſure hours of her ladies in this manner. See Lord Hales' *Annals of Scotland*, an. 1093.

V. 121. *Sir Knicht.*] "The addition *Sir* to the "names of knights was in uſe before the age of Ed- "ward I. and is from *Sire*, which in old French ſignifies "*Seignieur* or Lord. Though applicable to all knights "it ſerved properly to diſtinguiſh thoſe of the order "who were not barons." Dr. Stuart, *View of Society*, &c. Notes on ſect. 4. chap. ii. p. 269.

V. 123—128. The custom of the ladies tending the wounded knights was common in those romantic ages. *Lydgate*, whose story is ancient, but whose manners are those of his own times, has an instance in *The Story of Thebes*, part ii. Speaking of the daughter of Lycurgus and Tideus;

To a chamber she led him up aloft.
Full well beseine, there in a bed right soft,
Richly abouten apparrailed
With clothe of gold, all the floure irailed
Of the same both in length and brede:
And first this lady, of her womanhede,
Her women did bid, as goodly as they can,
To be attendant unto this wounded man:
And when he was unarmed to his shert,
She made first wash his woundis smert,
And serch hem well with divers instruments,
And made fet sundrie ointments, &c.

And in an excellent piece of old English poetry, styled Sir Cauline, published by Dr. Percy in the first volume of his *Reliques*, when the king is informed that knight is sick, he says,

Fetche me down my daughter deere,
She is a leeche fulle fine. v. 29, 30.

V. 145—152.] This ſtanza is now firſt printed. It is ſurpriſing it's omiſſion was not marked in the fragment formerly publiſhed, as without it the circumſtance of the knight's complaint is altogether foreign and vague. The loſs was attempted to be gloſſed over by many variations of the preceding four lines, but the defect was palpable to the moſt inattentive peruſer.

V. 154. *Lord Chattan.*] This is a very ancient and honourable Scottiſh ſurname. Some genealogiſts derive them from the *Chatti*, an ancient German tribe; but others, with more probability, from the *Gilchattan* of Ireland. St. *Chattan* was one of the firſt Scotiſh confeſſors, to whom was dedicated the priory of *Ardchattan* in Lorn, founded in 1230, and ſome others through the kingdom. The chief of the clan *Chattan* dying in the reign of David I. without male iſſue, the clan aſſumed the anceſtor of the *M'Pherſons* for ſuperior, by which means the name appears to have been loſt in that of *M'Pherſon.* See *Buchanan's Brief Enquiry into the Genealogy and Preſent State of Ancient Scottiſh Surnames.* Glaſgow, 1723, 4to, *p.* 67.

We however find the Clan Chattan mentioned as late as 1590 in *The Hiſtory of the Feuds and Conflicts of the Clans, publiſhed from a MS. of the reign of James VI.* Glaſgow, 1764; where a Macintoſh is called their chief.

V. 159.

V. 159.] Though we learn from *Buchanan's Equiry*, &c. that the clan *Chattan* are ſaid to have come into Scotland long before the expulſion of the Picts, yet I do not find this pretty anecdote, which is much in the ſpirit of Homer, has any foundation in hiſtory. The empire of the Picts was demoliſhed by Kenneth about four centuries before the apparent date of the events narrated in this poem.

V. 169. *Mak oriſons*, &c.] This is perfectly in the ſtyle of knighthood. Before they entered into combat they ſolemly invoked the aid of God, their Saviour, or their miſtreſs: religion and gallantry being the prime motives of all their adventures. *Les premieres leçons qu'on leur donnoit regardoient principalement l'amour de Dieu et des dames, c'eſt à dire la religion et la galanterie.* St. Palaye, tome i. p. 7. The poets of theſe times began, in like manner, the deſcription of a ſavage conflict, or of their lady's graces, with religious invocation. Many examples of which appear in the *Hiſtoire des Troubadours* of L'Abbé Milot, and the *Specimens of Welſh Poetry* publiſhed by Mr. Evans. So blind is the untutored mind to the proper diſcrimination of it's ideas!

V. 179. *Playand Pibrochs.*] Of the *pibroch* I cannot give a better account than in the words of an excellent author. ‘ A pibroch is a ſpecies of tune peculiar, I think, to the Highlands and Weſtern Iſles of Scotland. It is performed on a bagpipe, and differs totally from all other muſic. Its rythm is ſo irregu-

‘ lar,

'lar, and its notes, especially in the quick movement, 'so mixed and huddled together, that a stranger finds 'it almost impossible to reconcile his ear to it, so as to 'perceive its modulation. Some of these *pibrochs*, being 'intended to represent a battle, begin with a grave mo-'tion resembling a march, then gradually quicken into 'the onset; run off with noisy confusion, and turbu-'lent rapidity, to imitate the conflict and pursuit; 'then swell into a few flourishes of triumphant joy; 'and perhaps close with the wild and slow wailings of 'a funeral procession.' *Essays by Dr. Beattie*, 8vo. ed. p. 422. *note*.

V. 188. *Eir faes their dint mote drie.*] This is substituted in place of a line of consummate nonsense, which has stained all the former editions. Many such are corrected in this impression from comparing different rehearsals, and still more from conjecture. When an ignorant person is desired to repeat a ballad, and is at a loss for the original expression, he naturally supplies it with whatever absurdity first occurs to him, that will form a rime. These the Editor made not the smallest scruple to correct, as he always imagined that common sense might have its use even in emendatory criticism.

V. 203. *But on his forehead*, &c.] The circumstances in this description seem borrowed from those of different battles betwixt the Kings of Scotland and Norway. I find in no historian that Alexander was wounded in the battle of Largs; on the contrary, it is even doubted

whether

whether he was present; but in that near *Nairn* Malcolm II. was wounded on the head. *Rex, accepto in capite vulnere, vix a ſuis in propinquum nemus ablatus, ac ibi equo poſitus, mortem evaſit.* Buchan. lib. VI.

V. 223. *Hire dames to wail your darling's fall.*] This cuſtom of employing women to mourn for the warriors who fell in battle, may be traced to the moſt diſtant antiquity. Lucilius, one of the earlieſt Roman poets, in a couplet preſerved by Nonius, mentions this practice;

Mercede quæ conductæ flent alieno in funere præficæ
Multæ & capillos ſcindunt, & clamant magis.

Among the Northern nations it partook of their barbarity. 'Inter eas autem ceremonias a barbara gente 'acceptas fuiſſe et has, ut genas roderunt mulierculæ, 'hoc eſt unguibus faciem dilaniarent et *leſſum* facerent, 'id eſt ſanguinem e venis mitterent, doloris teſtandi 'ergo; id quod Germani patria voce dicunt, *Ein laſſu* '*thun oder haben.*' Elias Schedius *de Diis Germ.* Syng. II. c. 51. A ſimilar mode of teſtifying their grief for the death of their chiefs, ſtill obtains in the Highlands, as we are informed by Mr. Pennant in his amuſing *Tour in Scotland.*

V. 225. *Coſtly Jupe.*] This was the *Sagum*, or military veſt of the Gauls and Germans. Dr. Stuart has with curious ingenuity derived the ſcience of Blazonry from the ornaments which were in time added to them. *Ubi ſupra*, p. 286, 287.

Virgil

Virgil has a paſſage remarkably ſimilar to this, in deſcribing the habit of the Gauls, I think in ÆneidVIII.

> Aurea cæſaries illis, atque aurea veſtis
> Virgatis lucet ſagulis.

V. 219. *Beir Norſe that giſt*, &c.] This has been generally miſunderſtood: the meaning is, *Bear that gift to the King of Norway, and bid*, &c.

V. 239. 245.] Theſe vaunts are much in Homer's manner, and are finely characteriſtic. The obſcure metaphor which conveys them illuſtrates a beautiful remark of an ancient critic, That allegory has a ſublime effect when applied to threatning. Μεγαλεῖον δὲ τί ἐστιν καὶ ἡ Ἀλληγορία, καὶ μάλιστα ἐν ταῖς ἀπειλαῖς· οἷον ὡς ὁ Διονύσιος ὅτι, "οἱ τέττιγες αὐτοῖς ᾄσονται χάμοθεν. Demet. Phal. de Eloc. c. 99.

V. 265. *Whar lyke a fyre to hether ſet.*] This appoſite ſimile alludes to an ancient practice of the Scots, termed *Mure burning*. The progreſs of the flame was ſo quick, that many laws appear in their Acts of Parliament, prohibiting its being uſed when any corn was ſtanding on ground adjacent to the heath intended to be burnt, though at a conſiderable diſtance from the ſpot where the flame was kindled.

V. 285. *Sore taken he was, fey!*] *Fey* here ſignifies only indeed, *in fay*, or, in faith: it is commonly uſed by the old Scotiſh poets in a ſarcaſtic or ironical ſenſe.

V. 305.

V. 305. *On Norway's coast*, &c.] These verses are in the finest style of Ballad poetry. They have been well imitated by a modern writer, who seems indebted, for the best strokes of his first production, to a taste for such compositions:

> Ye dames of Denmark! even for you I feel,
> Who, sadly sitting on the sea-beat shore,
> Long look for Lords that never shall return,
>
> *Douglas*, Act III.

I cannot conclude my observations upon the description here given of the battle, without adding, that though perhaps not the most sublime, it is the most animated and interesting to be found in any poet. It yields not to any in Ossian for lively painting, nor to any in Homer for those little anecdotes and strokes of nature, which are so deservedly admired in that master. 'Poetry and Rhetoric,' says the author of an Enquiry into the origin of our Ideas of the Sublime and Beautiful, 'do not succeed in exact description so well 'as Painting does; their business is to affect rather by 'sympathy than imitation; to display rather the effect 'of things on the mind of the speaker, or of others, 'than to present a clear idea of the things themselves. 'This is their most extensive province, and that in 'which they succeed the best.' Will he forgive me if I offer this rude Scotish Poem as an example sufficiently illustrative of this fine remark?

V. 231.

V. 321. *Loud and chill blew the Westlin wind, &c.*] This storm is artfully raised by the magic of Poetry to heighten the terrible, which is soon carried to a degree not surpassed in any production ancient or modern. It will recall to the reader the like artifice employed in the most sublime passage of *Tasso's Gierusalemme*, end of Canto 7.; and of *Homer's Iliad*, VIII. ver. 161. of Mr. Pope's Translation.

V. 327. *Seimd new as black as mourning weid.*] It was anciently the custom on any mournful event to hang the castle gates with black cloth. This is alluded to here, and more particularly mentioned in an excellent modern Ballad, entitled *The Birth of St. George*, which displays no mean knowledge of the manners of chivalry:

But when he reached his castle gate
His gate was hung with black.

Reliques, Vol. III. p. 222.

HARDYKNUTE. Part II.

I HAVE given the ſtanzas now added the title of a Second Part, though I had no authority from the recital. The break formerly made here by accident ſeemed to call for this pauſe to the reader.

V. 115. *Penants.*] Theſe were ſmall banners charged with the arms of the owner, and ſometimes borne over the helm of the ancient knight by his ſquire, and, as would ſeem, even that of the prince, Earl, or Chief Baron, by his Baneret. See ver. 331. The Engliſh word is *penon:*

> And by his banner borne is his *penon,*
> Of gold full rich; in which there was ybete
> The minotaure that he wan in Crete,

Says Chaucer ſpeaking of Theſeus in *The Knight's Tale.*

V. 252. *Draffan's touirs.*] The ruins of Draffan-caſtle are in Lanarkſhire.—They ſtand upon a vaſt rock hanging over the *Nethan* (ſee v. 329.) which a little below runs into the *Clyde.* From this a houſe ſituated very nigh the ruins is called *Craignethan.* This caſtle is ſo ancient, that the country people there ſay it was built by the *Pechts,* which is their common way of expreſſing the *Picts.*

V. 273.

V. 273. *His balbrik.*] This term for a coat of mail occurs in *Blind Harry*. It was properly uſed for one compoſed of ſmall rings of ſteel which yielded to every motion of the warrior, and was the ſame with the *lorica hamata* of the Romans, ſo picturesquely deſcribed by Claudian:

Conjuncta per artem
Flexilis inductis hamatur lamina membris,
Horribilis viſu, credas ſimulacra moveri
Ferrea, cognatoque viros ſpirare metallo.

In Rufin. Lib. II.

V. 275. *Securit by a warloc auld,* &c.] The belief that certain charms might ſecure the poſſeſſor from danger in combat was common in dark ages. ‘ I know ‘ a ſong, by which I ſoften and enchant the arms of my ‘ enemies, and render their weapons of no affect,’ ſays *Odin* in his *Magic*. Northern Antiq. *Vol.* II. *p.* 217. Among the Longobards they were forbidden by a poſitive Law. ‘ Nullus Campio adverſus alterum pugna-‘ turus audeat ſuper ſe habere *herbas nec res ad maleficia* ‘ *pertinentes*, niſi tantum corona ſua, quæ conveniunt. ‘ Et ſi ſuſpicio fuerit quod eas occulte habeat, inquira-‘ tur per Judicem, et ſi inventæ fuerunt, rejiciantur. ‘ Poſt quam inquiſitionem, extendet manum ſuam ipſe ‘ in manu Patrini aut Colliberti ſui, ante judicem, ‘ dicens, ſe nullam rem talem ſuper ſe habere, deinde ad ‘ certamen prodeat’ *LL. Longob. apud L.Germ. J. Baſil. Herold.* A ſimilar notion obtained even in England, as appears from the oath taken in the Judicial Combat. ‘ A. de B. ye ſhall ſwere that ye have no *ſtone of virtue,* ‘ *nor hearb of virtue, nor charme, nor experiment, nor none* ‘ *othir enchauntment by you nor for you, whereby ye truſt* ‘ *the better to overcome C. de D. your adverſarie,* that ſhall ‘ come agens you within theſe liſts in his defence, nor ‘ that ye truſt in none othir thynge propirly bot in ‘ God, and your body, and your brave quarel. So God ‘ you help and all halowes, and the holy goſpells.’ *Apud* Dugdale, *Orig. Juridic. & Miſcell. Aulica, Lond.* 1702. *p.* 166. And we find in a moſt acute and ingenious treatiſe on the point of honour, written in the middle of the ſixteenth century, that this precaution was eſteemed neceſſary ſo late as that period. *Il Duello del Mutio Juſtinopolitano,* In Vineg. 1566. lib. II. c. 9. *De i maleficii et incante.* ‘ Et non ſenza ragione i moderni Padrini ‘ fanno ſpogliare i cavallieri, che hanno da entrare in ‘ battaglia, et iſcuotere, et diligentemente eſſaminare ‘ i loro panni, &c.’ Many inſtances occur in the accounts of the civil wars of France, and of the Netherlands: and more particularly in the very curious ſtory of *Gowrie's Conſpiracy,* publiſhed by James VI. at *Edinburgh,* 1600, 4to. ‘ His Majeſty having before his ‘ parting out of that towne, cauſed to ſearch the ſayde ‘ Earle of Gowries pockets, in caſe any letters that ‘ might further the diſcovery of that conſpiracie might ‘ be founde therein. But nothing was found in them, ‘ but a little cloſe parchment bag full of magical

‘ characters,

'characters, and wordes of enchantment, wherein it 'seemed that hee had put his confidence, thinking him-'self never safe without them, and therefore ever car-'ried them about with him; being also observed, that 'while they were upon him, his wound, whereof he 'died, bled not; but incontinent, after the taking of 'them away, the blood gushed out in great abundance, 'to the great admiration of all the beholders.' See likewise *Memoirs of the Affairs of Scotland, by David Moyses*, Edin. 1755. where this piece is reprinted *ver-batim*. Maister William Rynd, a servant of Lord Gowrie's, deposition in the same volume, *p.* 297, has singular anecdotes with regard to these *characters*.

V. 276. Fairy *charm*.] The word *fairy* seemes to have been accepted by the ancient English and Scotish poets for *supernatural*, or *enchanted*. So Chaucer speaking of *Cambuscan's* horse,

It was of fairie, as the peple semed.

Squires Tale, p. 1.

V. 362.] It was the priviledge of the knights to hide their faces with armour, so that it was impossible to distinguish any one from another, except by his *blazon*, which seems at first to have been displayed over them, but came at length to be painted on their shields, whence *Coats of Arms*. A *villein* was obliged to have his countenance uncovered in battle. This circumstance attended to will save our wonder at Hardyknute's not knowing Draſſan in the Firſt Part, and Draſſan's not perceiving Malcolm here till his ſpear tore off his viſor: though Rothſay knows Draſſan either from his wearing a *blazon* on his armour, or from his face being uncovered in order to breathe from the combat.

V. 389. *Cheir ye my* mirrie men, &c.] It ſhould have been remarked on the firſt appearance of this word, P. I. v. 199, that *mirrie* was anciently uſed in a very different ſenſe from its preſent. It ſignified *honeſt*, *true*, *faithful*, but no where *jovial*. King James VI. in his *Dæmonologie* MS. *pen. Edit.* 'Surelie the difference vul-'gaire put betwixt thame is verrie *mirrie*, *and in a man-'ner trew*.' p. 10. And again in p. 18. 'Many *honeſt* '*and mirrie* men.' In like manner Merlin's Prophecies are ſtyled '*Mirrie words*,' in that of Beid. *Proph. of Rymer*, &c.

V. 413. *Oh King of Hevin!*] This is a common appellation of the Deity with the more ancient Scottiſh Poets. *By Hevins King*, is the familiar oath of *Blind Harrie's* heroes.

V. 419. *By my Forbere's ſaul.*] Swearing by the ſouls of their anceſtors was another uſed mode in thoſe times. The greateſt thought this oath moſt ſtrong and honourable; probably becauſe it implied the ſouls of their forefathers were in heaven, and, as was then believed, might lend them a ſupernatural aid, if the intention of their oath was juſt and unblameable.

V. 421. '*Now mind your aith*,' &c.] This paſſage is obſcure: the meaning I apprehend is, that Draſſan had,

had, before the combat, exacted an oath of Allan his baneret, that he would slay him, should the necessity of his affairs demand this sacrifice. More willing to lose his own life than possibly to take that of his great antagonist, he commands Allan to fulfil his engagement, which, with all the heroic faith of those times, he does without a pause. The particular expression '*The* shynand 'blade' might lead us to imagine, that it was thought impossible to pierce the supposed enchanted armour, but with one particular weapon, likeways perhaps *charmed*.

V. 437. *Icolm.*] The Nunnery at Icolm, or Icolmkill, was one of the most noted in Scotland. The Nuns were of the order of *Augustine*, and wore a white gown, and above it a rocket of fine linen. *Spotiswood's Account of the Religious Houses in Scotland*, p. 509. The ruins of this nunnery are still to be seen, with many tombs of the Princesses; one of which bears the year 1000. *Martin's Western Islands*, p. 262.

I cannot conclude my remarks on this Poem without wasting one on the story of Mrs. Wardlaw. That this lady may have indeed received a MS. of it as mentioned in Dr. Percy's introductory note, is highly probable. Many valuable MSS. prepared for the press, have had a worse fate. But that she was the author of this capital composition, so fraught with science of ancient manners as the above notes testify, I will no more credit, than that the common people in Lanarkshire, who can repeat scraps of both the parts, are the authors of the passages they rehearse. That she did not refuse the name of being the original composer is a strange argument: would not the first poet in Europe think it added to his reputation? If conjecture may be allowed where proof must ever be wanting, I suspect, if we assign the end of the fifteenth century as the date of the antique parts of this noble production, we shall not greatly err; though at the same time the language must convince us that many strokes have been bestowed by modern hands.

Since the first publication of this volume, Sir David Dalrymple, Lord Hales, whose abilities have been so often, and so successfully, exerted in illustrating the antiquities of his country, to the law and the literature of which he is so great an ornament, has communicated to the Editor some notices with regard to this poem of Hardyknute, which shall here be laid before the reader, almost in his own words.

The following are extracts of a letter written by Sir John Bruce of Kinross, to Lord Binning, about the year 1719.

'To perform my promise, I send you a true copy of 'the manuscript I found, some weeks ago, in a vault 'at Dumferline. It is written on vellum in a fair 'Gothic character; but so much defaced by time, as 'you'll find that the tenth part is not legible.'

Sir John tranfcribes fome ftanzas, which he calls *verfes*. After l. 112, P. I. he fays, 'here are four 'verfes defaced,' and then he tranfcribes l. 113.

At l. 128 he adds, *hiatus in MS.* and then he tranfcribes l. 153. At l. 320 he fays, 'Here are ten verfes '(ftanzas) fo fpoilt that I can only guefs by the many 'proper names, that they contain the order of battle 'of the Scots army, as they ftood ranged under their 'different chieftains.'

In conclufion Sir John fays, 'there's a vaft deal more 'of it, but all defaced.'

The reader is left to judge whether this ftory of the manufcript on vellum, &c. has moft the appearance of a true narrative, or of a *jeu d' efprit* addreffed to a familiar friend.

Lord Hales has a copy of the original edition of Hardyknute, with MS. alterations, in the hand writing of Dr. John Clerk, Phyfician in Edinburgh. At l. 85, it has '*brade* Thomas;' Sir John Bruce has '*bred* Mal-'colm.' At l. 98, Sir John Bruce's MS. has 'Walter' inftead of 'Malcolm.' At l. 103, 'brazen' for 'filver;' and at l. 104, 'iron doors,' for 'painted 'bowers.'

In Dr. Clerk's MS. lines, 176—180 run thus;

To join his king adown the hill,
In haft his ftrides he bent;
While minftrels playand pibrochs fine,
Afore him ftately went.

In

In Dr. Clerk's MS. the ſtanza *On Norway's coaſt*, &c. comes in after the ſtanza *There on a lee* with much propriety: that reading is therefore followed in this edition.

At l. 337. for 'owr' the MS. has 'oy'.

The laſt line in the MS. was originally,

He feared a coud be feared;

but has been changed into that which occurs in later editions.

CHILD MAURICE.

THIS is undoubtedly the true title of this incomparable Ballad, though corrupted into Gil Morrice by the nurſes and old women, from whoſe mouths it was originally publiſhed. *Child* ſeems to have been of equal importance with *Damoiſeau* (See note on P. I. v. 49. of Hardyknute) and applicable to a young nobleman when about the age of fifteen. It occurs in Shakſpeare's Lear, in the following line, probably borrowed from ſome old romance or ballad,

Child Roland to the dark tower came.

Act III. S. 7.

And

And in Chaucer's *Rime of Sir Topas*, *Child* is evidently used to denote a young and noble knight. Many instances might likewise be brought from Spenser for this signification.

Gil Morrice is only the northern pronunciation of the true name of this ballad: *Gil* about Aberdeen, &c. still signifies *Child*, as it does in Galic; witness the name *Gilchrist*, the child of Christ, &c.

V. 52. *He bent his bow.*] Archery was enjoined the Scotish warrior at a very early age, as appears from many special laws to that effect, and particularly the following one of James I. 'Item, That all men busk 'them to be Archeres fra they be *twelfe yeir of age*, 'and that in ilk ten pundis worthe of lande their be 'maid bowmarkis, and speciallie neir to Paroche kirkis, 'quhairin upon haly daies men may cum, and at the 'leist schutte thrise about, and have usage of archerie: 'and quha sa usis not the said archerie, the Laird of 'the lande sall raise of him a wedder; and giff the 'Laird raises not the said payne, the King's schiresse or 'his ministers, shall raise it to the King.' *Parl.* I. § 18.

V. 95. *ezar.*] This word is perhaps the same with *mazer*, as used by the English poets,

A mighty mazer bowl of wine was set.

Spenser, F. Q. II. 12. 49.

A

A mazer ywrought of the maple ware,
Spenſer's Calendar, Auguſt.

So golden mazer wont ſuſpicion breed
Of deadly hemlocks poiſon'd potion :

ſays Hall in the prologue to his admirable Satires. *Ezar cup* will then mean a large bowl of any material.

V. 107, 8. *O what means a the folk coming? My mother tarries lang.*] This ſtroke of nature is delicate. It paints the very thought of youth and innocence. In ſuch happy *tenuity* of phraſe, this exquiſite compoſition is only rivalled by the *Merope* of *Maffei*, the moſt finiſhed Tragedy in the world. Some lines fancifully interpolated by a modern and very inferior hand are here omitted.

V. 122. *And ſtaided owr the ſtrae.*] The meaning is, *He went haſtily over the rank graſs.*

V. 144. *As the hip is o the ſtean.*] This would appear the corruption of ſome nurſe; but taking it as it ſtands, the ſimile, though none of the moſt delicate, has a parallel in the Father of Engliſh Poetry :

But he was chaſte and no lechoure
And ſweet as is the bramble floure
That bearethe the red hip.

Chaucer, Sir Topas.

ADAM

ADAM O GORDON.

THE genuine ſubject of this Ballad has long remained in obſcurity, though it muſt have been noted to every peruſer of *Crawford's Memoirs.*

'But to return to Gordon,' (*viz.* Sir Adam Gordon of Auchindown, brother to the Earl of Huntly) 'as 'theſe two actions againſt Forbes, or, to ſpeak more 'properly, againſt the rebels, gained him a vaſt repu'tation—his next exploit was attended with an equal 'portion of infamy; and he was as much decryed for 'this unlucky action (though at the ſame time he had 'no immediate hand in the matter) as for his former 'ones he had been applauded. He had ſent one *Captain* '*Ker* with a party of foot to ſummon the Caſtle of '*Towie* in the Queen's name. The owner Alexander 'Forbes was not then at home, and his lady confiding 'too much in her ſex, not only refuſed to ſurrender, 'but gave Ker very injurious language; upon which, 'unreaſonably tranſported with fury, he ordered his 'men to fire the caſtle, and barbarouſly burnt the 'unfortunate gentlewoman with her whole family, 'amounting to thirty-ſeven perſons. Nor was he ever 'ſo much as caſhiered for this inhuman action, which 'made Gordon ſhare both in the ſcandal and the guilt.' *An.* 1571. *p.* 240. *edit.* 1706.

In this narrative is immediately perceived every leading circumſtance in the Ballad. The *Captain Car*, by which name it was diſtinguiſhed in Dr. Percy's Manuſcript, is evidently the *Ker* of Crawford. The Houſe of *Rodes* I have corrected, according to the truth of ſtory, *Towie*. Of which name, I find in *Gordon of Straloch's* map of Aberdeenſhire, there were two gentlemen's ſeats, or caſtles, in his time, one upon the *Don*, and another upon the *Ythan*. The neareſt ſeat to the latter is that of *Rothy*, which from wrong information may have originally ſtood in the Ballad, the miſtake riſing naturally from the vicinity of their ſituation, and from this have been corrupted to *Rodes*. The courage of this lady, as repreſented in the Ballad, was equalled by that of the famous Counteſs of Saliſbury, at the ſiege of Roxborough; and of Ladies Arundel and Banks, in the laſt civil wars of England. See particularly the *Mercurius Ruſticus*, &c. Lond. 1647. Sections V. and XI.

V. 129. *Freits.*] This word ſignifies *ill omens*; and ſometimes as here *Accidents ſupernaturally unlucky*. King James VI. in his *Dæmonologie*, *MS. pen. Edit.* B. I. *ch.* IIII. *p.* 13. 'But I pray you forget not likeways 'to tell what are the Devill's rudimentis. E. His ru-'dimentis I call firſt in generall all that quhilk is called 'vulgairelie the vertu of woode, herbe, and ſtaine; 'quhilk is uſed by unlawfull charmis without naturall 'cauſis. As lykeways all kynd of prattiques, *freitis*, *or*

'uther

'*uther lyk extraordinair actions, quhilk cannot abyde the trew*
'*twiche of naturall raison.*' It occurs again in the same sense in *p.* 14. *marg. note*; and in *p.* 41. speaking of *Sorcerers.* 'And in generall that naime was gevin 'thaime for using of sic chairmis and *freitis*, as that 'craft teachis thame.'

THE CHILD OF ELLE.

THIS ballad is admitted into this collection, as being supposed, from many minute marks, to be a Scotish ballad in an English dress. *Whan* for *when*, *kirk* for *church*, &c. are some of these marks.

Though it is published by Dr. Percy, and of consequence in every body's hands; yet it was necessary to give it here, else this digest of such Scotish tragic ballads as deserve preservation could not have been called complete.

VI.

John Faw was king of the gypsies in Scotland in the reign of James IV. who, about the year 1495, issued a proclamation, ordaining all sheriffs, &c. to assist John Faw in seizing and securing fugitive gypsies; and that they should lend him their prisons, stocks, fetters, &c. for that purpose: charging the lieges, that none of them molest, vex, unquiet, or trouble the said Faw and

and his company in doing their *lawful business* within the realm; and in their passing, remaining, or going forth of the same, under penalty: and charging skippers, masters of ships, and mariners, within the realm, at all ports and havens, to receive said John and his company, upon their expences, for furthering them furth of the realm to parts beyond sea. See *Mr. Maclaurin's Remarkable Cases*, &c. *p.* 774.

V. 8. *Glamour.*] The *glamour* was believed to be a kind of magical mist raised by sorcerers, which deluded their spectators with visions of things which had no real existence, altered the appearance of these which really did exist, &c. The Eastern nations have a similar superstition, as we may learn from Mr. Galland's *Mille et un nuit*, and other translations of works of Oriental fiction.

SIR HUGH, OR THE JEW'S DAUGHTER,

is composed of two copies, one published by Dr. Percy, the other in a collection of Scotish Songs, &c. *Edin.* 1776. The *Mirryland toun* of the former, and *Mirry Linkin* of the latter, evidently shew that the noted story of Hugh of Lincoln is here expressed.

FLODDEN FIELD.

THE ſtanzas here given form a complete copy of this exquiſite Dirge. The inimitable beauty of the original induced a variety of verſifiers to mingle ſtanzas of their own compoſure. But it is the painful, though moſt neceſſary duty of an Editor, by the touch-ſtone of truth, to diſcriminate ſuch droſs from the gold of antiquity.

SIR PATRICK SPENCE

is given from Dr. Percy's Edition, which indeed agrees with the ſtall copies, and the common recitals. I have, however, lent it a few corrections, where palpable abſurdity ſeemed to require them. The phraſe in v. 25. of ſeeing the old moon *in the arms* of the new is ſtill familiar in Scotland. It means that the opaque part of the moon's diſk caſts a glimmering light, while the illuminated part is waxing; and is to this hour eſteemed to prognoſticate a ſtorm.

LADY BOTHWELL's LAMENT.

THESE four ſtanzas appeared to the Editor to be all that are genuine in this elegy. Many additional ones are to be found in the common copies, which are rejected as of meaner execution. In a quarto manuſcript in the Editor's poſſeſſion, containing a collection of Poems by different hands from the reign of Queen Elizabeth to the middle of the laſt century, when it was apparently written (*pp.* 132.) there are two *Balowes* as they are there ſtyled, the firſt *The Balow, Allan*, the ſecond *Palmer's Balow*; this laſt is that commonly called Lady Bothwell's Lament, and the three firſt ſtanzas in this edition are taken from it, as is the laſt from *Allan's Balow*. They are injudiciouſly mingled in Ramſay's Edition, and ſeveral ſtanzas of his own added; a liberty he uſed much too often in printing ancient Scotiſh poems.

EARL OF MURRAY.

V. laſt. *Toun.*] This word is often uſed in Scotland to denote only, perhaps, a farm-houſe and office-houſes, or a number of hovels ſcattered here and there; and on which the Engliſh would not beſtow the name of a village.

A very eminent Scotish antiquary informs me, that in Saxon *ton* signifies an habitation: and that *castle downe* in the last stanza of this ballad ought to be read *Castle Downe*, the seat of Lord Murray in his own right.

SIR JAMES THE ROSE

is given from a modern edition in one sheet 12mo. after the old copy. A renovation of this Ballad, composed of new and improbable circumstances, decked out with scraps of tragedies, may be found in the Annual Register for 1774, and other collections. *Rose* is an ancient and honourable name in Scotland: *Johannes de Rose* is a witness to the famous Charter of *Robert* II. testifying his marriage with *Elizabeth More*, as appears in the rare edition of it printed at Paris, 1695, 4to. *p.* 15.

V. 27. *Belted Knights.*] The *belt* was one of the chief marks which distinguished the ancient knight. *To be girt with the belt of knighthood* often implied the whole attending ceremonies which constituted that order. That of the common knight was of white leather.

LAIRD OF WOODHOUSELIE.

THIS Ballad is now first published. Whether it has any real foundation, the Editor cannot be positive, though it is very likely. There is a *Woodhouselie* nigh Edinburgh, which may possibly be that here meant.

LORD LIVINGSTON

was probably an ancestor of Livingston Earl of Linlithgow, attainted in 1715. This affecting piece likewise, with the four following, now appears for the first time.

V. 13. *Swith dreams are scant*] This seems a proverbial expression; King James in his *Dæmonologie*, 'That 'is *a swith dream* (as they say) sence thay see it walking.' *MS. p.* 100.

BINNORIE.

V. 32. *Her wraith.*] 'And what meanis then these 'kyndis of spreitis when they appeare in the shaddow 'of a personne newlie dead, or to die, to his friend? 'E. When thay appeare upon that occasion, they are 'called *wraithis* in our langage.' *Ib. p.* 81.

The following larger extract relating to the Fairies, another creation of superstition, is given by way of specimen of this singular MS. Book III. Ch. 5.

ARGU-

ARGUMENT.

'The description of the fourth kynde of Spreitis. 'called the *Pharie*. What is possible thairin, and what 'is but illusions. Whow far this dialogue entreates of 'all thir thingis: and to what ende.'

'*P.* Now I pray you come on to that fourt kynd of 'spreittis. *E.* That fourt kynde of Spreitis, quhilk be 'the gentiles was called Diana and her wandring court, 'and amongs us was called the *Pharie* (as I tolde you) 'or our guid neighbouris' (the King has added on the margin 'or sillie wightis') 'was ane of the fortis of 'allusions that was rysest in tyme of Papistrie; for all- 'though it was holdin odious to prophesie be the devill, 'yet whome these kynd of spreittis caried away, and 'informed, thay wer thought to be sonciest, and of 'best lyfe. To speak of the manie vaine tratlis foundit 'upon that illusion; how thair was ane king and queine 'of *Pharie*, of sic a jolie court and traine as thay had; 'how thay had a teind and a dewtie, as it wer, of all 'guidis: how thay naturallie raid and yeid, eat and 'drank, and did all other actions lyke naturall men 'and wemen; I think it is lyker Virgilis *Campi Elisei*, 'nor any thing that aught to be beleived be Chris- 'tianis.'

This Manuscript is written in a beautiful Italic hand, so nearly resembling copper-plate engraving, as to have been taken for such even after accurate examination. It is bound in gilded vellum, stamped with the King's cypher beneath the crown; and is in all probability the original copy of this royal monument of superstition. Many additions are inserted on the margin, as would seem, of the hand-writing of James VI. and some notes for his own private use. As for instance on *B.* II. *ch.* 1. speaking of the Magicians of his time, over against the words 'Thay are sume of thame riche and worldlie 'wyse,' he has noted *F. M.* 'sum of tham fat or cor-'pulent in their bodies,' *R. G.* 'and maist pairt of 'thame altogethir gevin ouer to the pleasours of the 'flesche,' *B. N.*

We need not wonder at the severity with which the imaginary crime of withcraft was punished in his reign, when we remark his sentiment expressed on this head, in *B.* III. *ch.* 6. of this singular tract. '*P.* Then 'to make ane ende of our conference sence I see it 'drawis leatt, what forme of punishment think ye 'merites thir Magiciens and Witches? For I see that 'ye account thame to be all alyke giltie. E. *(The King.)* '*Thay aught to be put to deathe*, according to the law of 'God, the civill and imperiall law, and the municipal 'law of all Christiane nations. *P.* But what kynde of 'death I pray you? *E.* It is commonly used be fyre, 'but that is ane indifferent thing to be used in every 'countrey according to the law or custume thairof. *P.* '*But aught no sexe, aage, nor rank, to be eximed?* E. 'NONE AT ALL.'

The

The language of this pedantic Monarch is particular; it is that of a Scotish school-boy beginning to read English.

In the printed copies the style is much altered and improved. It was printed at Edinburgh, and re-printed at London in the same year, 1603, 4to.

LORD AIRTH's COMPLAINT.

THESE verses, though somewhat uncouth, are moving, as they seem to flow from the heart. They are now first published from the Editor's quarto Manuscript, *p.* 16. corrected in some lines, which appeared too inaccurate for the publick eye. Two entire stanzas are rejected from the same cause. I know nothing of the nobleman to whom they are ascribed.

In the same Manuscript (*p.* 17. and 116) are to be found the two following Poems, which I believe have never been in print. They are here added, with a few corrections. They were both written by Sir Robert Aytoun, who bore some office under government in the reign of James VI. if I mistake not. His Latin poems are in the Delitiæ Poetarum Scotorum.

S O N N E T.

WILT thou, remorseless fair, still laugh while I lament?
Shall still thy chief contentment be to see me malcontent?
Shall I, Narcissus like, a flying shadow chase?
Or, like Pygmalion, love a stone crown'd with a winning face?
No, know my blind Love now shall follow Reason's eyes;
And as thy fairness made me fond, thy temper make me wise.
My loyalty disdains to love a loveless dame,
The spirit still of Cupid's fire consists in mutual flame.
Hadst thou but given one look, or hadst thou given one smile,
Or hadst thou lent but one poor sigh my sorrows to beguile,
My captive Thoughts perchance had been redeem'd from Pain,
And these my mutinous Discontents made friends with Hope again.
But thou I know at length art careless of my good;
And wouldst ambitiously embrew thy beauty in my blood:
A great disgrace to thee, to me a monstrous wrong,
Which time may teach thee to repent ere haply it be long:
But to prevent thy shame, and to abridge my woe,
Because thou canst not love thy friend, I'll cease to love my foe.

SONG.

SONG.

WHAT means this ſtrangeneſs now of late,
 Since Time muſt Truth approve?
This diſtance may conſiſt with ſtate,
 It cannot ſtand with love.

'Tis either cunning or diſtruſt
 That may ſuch ways allow:
The firſt is baſe, the laſt unjuſt;
 Let neither blemiſh you.

For if you mean to draw me on,
 There needs not half this art:
And if you mean to have me gone,
 You over-act your part

If kindneſs croſs your wiſh'd content,
 Diſmiſs me with a frown;
I'll give you all the love that's ſpent,
 The reſt ſhall be my own.

FRAGMENTS.

The two firſt of theſe are given from a Collection, Edinburgh, 1776, but poliſhed by the preſent Editor; the two others from recital.

GLOS-

GLOSSARY.

A

Ablins, *perhaps.*
Aboon, *above.*
Ae, ane, *one.*
Aff, *off.*
Aft, *oft.*
Aith, *oath.*
Ain, *own.*
Alſe, *except.*
Anes, *once.*
Auld, *old.*
Auſterne, *ſtern.*
Ayont, *beyond.*

B

Ba, *ball, tennis.*
Baird, *beard.*
Baith, *both.*
Bairn, *child.*
Bale, *miſery.*
Balow, *huſh.*
Band, *ſolemn oath.*
Baſe-court, *bas court,* French, *the lower court of a caſtle.*
Baſnet, *helmet.*
Begyle, *beguile.*
Beſtraught, *diſtracted.*
Banſters, *bluſterers.*
Beik, *baſk.*
Belyve, *immediately.*
Beſprent, *covered.*
Betide, n. *fortune.*
Bedeen, *preſently,*
Bleiſe, *blaze.*
Bleirit, *dim with tears.*
Blink, *glimpſe of light.*
Blinking, *twinkling.*
Blude, *blood.*
Blythſum, *ſprightly.*
Boughts, *ſheepfolds.*
Boiſt, *boaſt.*
Bonny, *pretty.*
Botand, *likeways.*
Bown, *make ready.*
Bogle, *hobgoblin.*
Bot, *without.*
Bouir, *a room arched in the Gothic manner.*
Bouir woman, *chamber-maid.*
Bra, *bravely dreſſed.*
Brae, *ſide of a hill.*
Braid, *broad.*
Brand, Iſl. *a ſword.*
Brawe, *brave.*
Brayd, *haſten.*
Bruik, *enjoy.*
Brin, *burn.*

Brig.

Brig, *bridge.*
Busk, *prepare.*
Brechan, *plaid; cloke striped with various colours.*

C

Cauld, *cold.*
Cauldrif, *chill, damp.*
Canny, *prudent.*
Cheis, *chuse.*
Claught, *grasped.*
Cliding, *wardrobe.*

D

Daffin, *waggery.*
Dar'd, *lighted, bit.*
Darrain, *suffer, encounter.*
Deft, *taken off hastily.*
Dint, *blow, stroke.*
Dawning, *dawn of day.*
Dought, *could.*
Doughty, *valiant, strong.*
Dowie, *dreadful, melancholy.*
Drie, *suffer, endure.*
Dule, *grief.*

E

Eard, *earth.*
Eild, *eld, old age.*
Eine, *eyes.*
Eithly, *easily.*
Eydent, *ayding, assisting.*
Elrie, *dismal.*
Eldern, *ancient, venerable.*
Egre, *eager, keen, sharp.*
Effray, *affright.*
Emraud, *Emerald.*
Ettle, *aim.*

F

Fae, *foe.*
Fay, *faith, sincerity.*
Fere, *companion.*
Ferly, *wonder.*
Feid, *enmity.*
Fey, *in sooth.*
Flinders, *splinters.*
Fleeching, *flattering.*
Forbere, *forefather, ancestor.*
Forbode, *denial.*
Frae, *fro, from.*
Frawart, *froward.*

G

Ga, gae, gang, *go.*
Gabbing, *prattle.*
Gait, *way, path.*
Gar, *cause.*
Gie, *give.*
Gin, gif, *if.*
Glaive, *sword.*
Gleit, *glittered.*
Glie, *mirth. In* H. P. II. 120. *it seems to signify a faint light.*
Glent, *glanced.*
Glist, *glistered.*
Gloming, *dusk.*
Glowr, *glare, dismal light.*
Grein, *desire.*
Greit, *weep.*

Graith,

Graith, *dress*, v. *and* n.
Gousty, *ghastly*.
Grie, *prize*, *victory*.
Gude, *good*.
Gurly, *bitter*, *cold*; *applied to weather*.
Gyle, *guile*.
Gyse, *manner*, *fashion*.

H

Harst, *harvest*.
Hauld, *hold*, *abode*.
Hain, *spare*, *save*.
Hap, *cover*.
Hecht, *promised*.
Hip, *the berry of the wild rose*.
Hyt, *frantic*.
Hynd, *hence*.

I

Jimp, *delicate*, *slender*.
Ilk, ilka; *each*.
Irie, *terrible*.

K

Kaming, *combing*.
Kin, *kindred*.
Kyth, v. *to show or make appear*.
Kyth, n. *acquaintance*, *friends*, *companions*.

L

Laigh, *low*.
Lane, *alone*.
Lap, *leaped*.
Law, *low*.
Lave, *the rest*.
Leil, *true*, *faithful*.
Leir, *learn*.
Leglen, *a milking pail*.
Leman, *lover*, *mistress*.
Leugh, *laughed*.
Lawing, *reckoning*.
Lever, *rather*.
Leech, *physician*.
Lift, *the firmament*.
Lig, *lye scatteredly*.
Lilting, *merry making with music*, &c.
Lin, *a fall of water*.
Linkis, *lamps or other artificial lights*.
Loaning, *a common green near a village*.
Loch, *lake*.
Low, v. *and* n. *flame*.
Lown, *sheltered*, *calm*.
Lout, *to bow*.
Lue, *love*.
Lure, *cunning device*, *snare*.
Lyart, *hoary*.

M

Makless, *matchless*.
Maun, *must*.
Mair, *more*, s. *rather*.
Mahoun, *Mahomet*, *and by abuse the devil*.
Mane, *moan*, *lament*.
Meikle, *much*.

Meiny,

Meiny, *train, army.*
Mense, *to measure, to try.*
Mede, *reward.*
Meid, *port, appearance.*
Meise, *soften, mollify.*
Mirk, *dark.*
Mony, *many.*
Mote, *might.*

N

Na, nae, *no, none.*
Neist, *next*
Norse, *often* the King of Norway, *so* France *is often used by Shakspere for the king of that country.*

O

On case, *perhaps.*
Ony, *any.*
Or, s. *ere, before,* s. *else.*
Owr, *Over.*
Outowr, *Over above.*
Orison, Fr. *prayer.*

P

Pall, *robe of state.*
Payne, *penalty.*
Perle, *pearl.*
Pleasance, *pleasure.*
Pou, *pull.*
Pratique, *experiment.*
Preass, *to press, to pass with difficulty.*
Prime of day, *dawn.*
Prive, pruve, *prove.*
Propine, *reward.*

Q

Qu, *is used in old Scotish spelling for* W. *as* Quhat, *What,* &c.
Quat, *quitted.*
Quell, *subdue.*

R

Raught, recht, *reached.*
Recule, *recoil.*
Rede, *warn.*
Reiking, *smoking.*
Rief, *robbery.*
Riever, *robber,*
Reid, *red.*
Roun, *sound softly, whisper.*
Rue, *repent.*
Ruth, *pity.*
Rude, *cross.*
Runkled, *wrinkled.*

S

Sark, *shirt.*
Saw, *a wise saying.*
Sawman, *counsellor.*
Sabbing, *sobbing.*
Scant, *scarce.*
Scorning (*Flod.* v. 5.) *jesting ironicaly.*
Sey, *essay, try.*
Seen, *to see.*
Seim, *appearance.*

Selcouth,

Selcouth, *uncommon as a prodigy.*
Share, *to cleave, pierce.*
Sic, *such.*
Sindle, *seldom.*
Skaith, *hurt.*
Slaid, *to move speedily.*
Slee, v. *slay.*
Sen, *seeing.*
Sin, sith, *since.*
Soncie, *lucky.*
Stalwarth, *stout, valiant.*
Steik, *to shut.*
Sleuth, *sloth.*
Strecht, *stretched.*
Swankies, *merry fellows.*
Swaird, *turf, grassy ground.*
Swith, *quickly.*
Steid, *estate.*
Spent, *drew.*
Splent, *armour for the thighs and legs.*
Speir, *ask.*
Stoup, *pillar.*
Sucred, *sugared.*
Syre, *lord.*

T

Tane, *taken.*
Targe, *shield.*
Tein, *sorrow.*
Teind, *tyth, tenth part.*
Thilk, thir, *these.*
Thole, *suffer, permit.*
Thud, *sudden noise.*
Tide, *time, season.*
Tint, *lost.*
Triest, *make an assignation.*
Twin'd, *parted, separated.*

V U

Veir, *avoid*, or perhaps *alter.*
Unmusit, *without wonder*; to muse *often means* to wonder *in Shakspere.*
Unsonsie, *unlucky.*

W

Waddin, *strong, firm.*
Wad, wald, wold; *would.*
Warloc, *wizard.*
Wallow, *withered*, and fig. *pale.*
Ward, *sentinel.*
Wate, *warrand.*
Wax, *to spread, to become famous.*
Wee, *little.*
Weit, *wet, rain.*
Wete, *hope.*
Westlin, *western.*
Wae worth ye, *woe befall you.*
War, *aware.*
Whilk, *which.*
Wighty, *strong.*
Wicht, *from* Wiga *Sax.* *a hero, or great man.*
Winsum, *agreeable, winning.*
Whyle, *until.*

Weir,

Weir, *war.*
Weily, *full of whirlpools; a weil is still used for a whirlpool in the west of Scotland.*
Wraith, *a spirit or ghost.*
Wyte, *blame.*
Wreak, *revenge.*
Wreken, *avenged.*
Wreuch, *grief, misery.*

Y

Yestreen, *the evening of yesterday.*
Yet, *gate,*
Yied, *went.*
Youthheid, *state of youth.*

THE END.

www.ingramcontent.com/pod-product-compliance
Lightning Source LLC
Chambersburg PA
CBHW030116030726
47498CB00007B/2410

9783744766654